To Cari

Enjoy - secrets.

Val x.

STORY OF A COUNTRY BOY

Val Portelli

It's a long and exciting road from an insular country village to the temptations of Swinging Sixties London, but one TJ is determined to experience to the full.

Good looks and wild dancing abilities smooth his path through the seedier side of Soho life, as he seeks to achieve his dreams - if only he knew what they were.

Follow his journey and decide for yourself where his heart truly lies.

© 2019 Val Portelli
First edition Published 2019
Publishers: Quirky Unicorn Publications
www.QuirkyUnicornBooks.wordpress.com

This book is recommended for adults only, and might not be considered suitable for children.

The moral right of the author has been asserted. All rights reserved. Apart from any fair dealing for the purpose of research or private study, or criticism or review, as permitted under the Copyright, Designs and Patents Act 1988, no part of this publication may be reproduced, stored or transmitted, in any form or by any means, without the prior permission in writing of the publishers, or in the case of reprographic reproductions in accordance with the terms of licences issued by the Copyright Licensing Agency.

Enquiries concerning reproduction outside these terms should be sent to the publishers.

This book is sold subject to the condition that it shall not, by way of trade or otherwise, be lent, resold, hired out, or otherwise circulated without the publisher's prior consent in any form of binding or cover other than that in which it is published and without a similar condition being imposed on the subsequent purchaser. This is a work of fiction. Names, characters, businesses, places events and incidents are either the product of the author's imagination or used in a fictitious manner. Any resemblance to actual persons, living or dead, or actual events is purely coincidental.

Acknowledgements
Book cover artist and beta reader: Paula Harmon.
Editing:
www.jeanfonkemproofedit.com/services
Inspiration: The author's imagination, the island of Malta and the area of Soho, London.

About the author

www.amazon.com/Voinks/e/B01MVB8WNC

www.amazon.co.uk/Val-Portelli/e/B01MVB8WNC

Table of Contents

Chapter One	1
Chapter Two	4
Chapter Three	7
Chapter Four	12
Chapter Five	17
Chapter Six	21
Chapter Seven	30
Chapter Eight	33
Chapter Nine	39
Chapter Ten	42
Chapter Eleven	46
Chapter Twelve	55
Chapter Thirteen	64
Chapter Fourteen	68
Chapter Fifteen	76
Chapter Sixteen	84
Chapter Seventeen	87
Chapter Eighteen	90
Chapter Nineteen	94

Chapter Twenty	100
Chapter Twenty-one	105
Chapter Twenty-two	109
Chapter Twenty-three	114
Chapter Twenty-four	119
Chapter Twenty-five	125
Chapter Twenty-six	131

Story of a Country Boy

Chapter One

The other villagers kept their front parlours under dust covers unless there was a wedding or a funeral - ours was given over to my father's pigs. It was normal in rural communities in those days to have numerous children and ours was no exception. There were eleven of us in the family, and although my mother had once been a beautiful woman, constant years of child-bearing had given her the appearance of an old lady.

Papa was the local baker. He was quiet and hard-working, baking cakes for christenings or other special occasions, and supplying everyone in the local community with bread six days a week. Even on Sundays he didn't rest. After attending early morning mass, he would fire up the ovens, and be ready to take the cloth covered dishes from the women in the village. Cooking facilities in the houses were basic, and as few had a proper oven, it was left to Papa to roast the slabs of lamb or beef in his kiln. The joints would come from the animals reared in their fields, or the chickens fed on scraps in the back gardens, in order to feed their extended families. For a few pennies he would cook the meat prepared for the traditional Sunday lunch, which even the married sons and daughters were expected to attend. It was only after all the cooking dishes had been collected that we would be able to sit and eat our own dinner. During the week the usual meal would be a constantly topped-up stew pot, made with home grown vegetables heated over an open fire.

      It was almost impossible for the younger generation to save enough money to buy their own property, the girls were carefully chaperoned, and the boys expected to choose a decent local girl, whose family was known and respected. Anyone not from the immediate community was treated as a foreigner; even the inhabitants of the closest villages were suspect. If a young man took a fancy to a girl from elsewhere, he would have a hard time convincing the family she would be worthy of becoming his bride. The mother ruled the roost at home, but the father's word was law, and the children did as they were told or suffered the consequences. Grandparents expected their own children to look after them in their dotage, and the old ladies liked nothing better than to sit in the shade by the front step, their arthritic fingers busy with knitting or making traditional lace, while they gossiped.

'You think your boy is a problem. Wait until he gets married and you have his wife to teach. I don't know what Grace's mother was thinking of. The girl hasn't a clue about how to wash and fold the sheets. And her timpana is a joke. I'll never know what my Phillip saw in her.'

'These youngsters are all the same. You should have seen the carry-on when I told Rita to wring the chicken's neck. All squeals and swoons as if she might break a finger-nail. Well, what do you expect if they marry a townie? Stick to your own kind, that's what I say.'

The shortcomings of the modern generation were a favourite topic, especially the inadequacies of their own daughters-in-law, unless of course, the mother of the girl in question was within hearing distance.

Chapter Two

Papa was a frugal man living a simple life, and over the years gradually built up a small nest egg. We never lacked for food, and compared to some of our neighbours, were comparatively well off, but it was not enough for me. There was no point being the largest fish in a tiny pond, when the world offered extensive rivers and immense oceans. As a small island we were surrounded by sea, but neither the prospect of being a fisherman, or working in the fields appealed. The only time I wanted to be on water was as the owner of a luxury yacht, sipping champagne and surrounded by beautiful women.

I was born during the war years, but being so young had little memory of the devastation and hardship my country endured. Due to its important location in the centre of the Mediterranean our island had been bombarded, but with habitual stubborn pride and resilience we rebuilt, and reverted to our traditional ways. As a colony, it was the continued presence of a garrison which changed the insular peace of the village forever, and had an unexpected and major impact on the way my life turned out. With hundreds of extra mouths needing their daily rations of bread, Papa became a comparatively rich man.

As the eldest son, my job was to take the horse and cart and deliver the fresh bread to the bases, but unlike my father I had no respect for hard work. Labouring all hours for a few pennies was not for me. I might have been an illiterate peasant but I had dreams. No one sneered or called me ignorant; my explosive temper saw to that.

'Hey, TJ. Be careful the troops don't chop up that haggard old nag for dinner. It's a long walk home.'

'Yeah, you think you're something because your dad doesn't get his hands dirty. Perhaps the soldiers can teach you how to be a man instead of a delivery boy.'

Sniggering, the two kids took off when they saw me jump down from the cart, but they were not quick enough. I caught up and beat them, first with my fists, and then with one of the metal poles from the baskets until they screamed for mercy. For good measure I climbed back onto the cart and heard the satisfying snap of broken bone as I drove the horse over the out-stretched leg sprawled in the dust in front of me. There was no point in continuing my journey; the bread that hadn't fallen in the dirt was covered with blood from the gash on my arm.

'Why are you back so soon? What's happened to the loaves?' My father was more concerned about his lost income than whether I had been hurt. 'Have you been fighting again?'

'No Papa. Some gunfire spooked the horse and he bolted. I hurt my arm trying to control him.'

'That's a day's work lost. Perhaps I should speak to the Commander and report it.'

'No Papa. They might get upset and stop their orders, then where would you be?'

As usual, Mama tried to come to my rescue as she saw my father reaching for his belt. 'He's right, Nino. Best let it lie. Come inside TJ and I'll see to that cut. You're dripping blood everywhere and the horse needs cleaning up. Freddie! See to the animal while I sort out your brother.'

Chapter Three

Papa kept his savings rolled up in elastic bands, but I was crafty and learnt to spy on him when he counted the profit from the day's takings, before returning the bundle to its hiding place. Even if there had been a bank in the village, few would have used it. Cash was all they knew, like their fathers and grandfathers before them. I couldn't understand why he hoarded his money. I wanted to be rich now, not when I was too old to enjoy it.

He was not an educated man but seemed to instinctively know when to start a new packet to make it easier to count. I never took a whole bundle, but would peel off one note from each roll in the hope he wouldn't notice. Although there was nowhere in the village to spend the stolen money, I needed it to prove I had more than the other boys.

My opportunity came when a farmer in a nearby parish put a horse up for sale. I bought it, but not as a pet. Animals were usually reared to work, to sell at the market, or for the food table, so it was pointless to give it a name. I rode him home and left him to graze in the field behind our house while I tried to come up with excuses.

'What do you mean it's "your" horse? You're only thirteen. Where would you get that sort of money?' Papa demanded when he saw it.

'I won it fair and square. Now leave me alone,' I shouted back, and then ran when I saw him pick up the thick, leather strap. I had inherited his temper, but I knew if I pushed him too far it was best to stay out his way until he had a chance to cool down. After dark I crept back home, and my mother quietly opened the door to let me in.

'He's asleep now, but I've never seen him so angry before. Why can't you be like the others, and just do as you're told? He's a good man and we both love you, but sometimes you're enough to try the patience of a saint. I'll talk to him in the morning and try to sort something out, but please try to show him more respect. All I'm asking for is some peace, without you constantly at each other's throats. Now get yourself off to bed, and try not to wake your brothers and sisters.'

I don't know what she said to persuade him but I was allowed to keep my horse. Our old mare was no longer able to make the long journey to the camps, and a week later was sent off to the slaughterhouse. At least I now had a young, fit animal when I visited the army barracks every day to sell Papa's produce. He had never visited them himself, and if it hadn't been for a couple of soldiers straying into our village and discovering the bakery by accident, the lucrative idea of supplying the troops would never have occurred to him. The squaddies made all the arrangements and I was designated to be the delivery boy. The furthest Papa had ever ventured was the village club, so I doubt he was even aware of the places springing up to cater for the worldly-wise foreigners.

Despite my youth, I bluffed my way into the dive bars, and for some reason the soldiers took to me. They opened the eyes of this flash, naïve, local boy to the big, bad world outside the rural community. I was a quick learner and by the time I was fifteen could hold my own, drinking and partying with the best of them. My life wouldn't have been worth living if Papa had discovered my existence as a delivery boy was way behind me, and most of his produce ended up dumped in a field, or sold wholesale at a generous discount. Gambling and stealing provided sufficient cash to keep him quiet, with enough left over for me to buy drinks in the sleazy clubs and bars.

Even in the 1950s our village girls were chaperoned until they were safely married off. The foreign girls were different. I was an excellent dancer and with my curly hair, good looks and natural exuberance, became a popular favourite with the ladies in the military camps and bars. I had lost my virginity at fourteen to a local older prostitute who had taken pity on me, but despite my inexperience was a willing pupil when the sophisticated, worldly women taught me how to bring them pleasure.

The good life came to an end when I was arrested for stealing, shortly after my seventeenth birthday. I was locked up, but surprisingly my father put up the money to secure my release. In the few months it took for him to grease the right palms I furthered my education from the hardened inmates. I came out of prison with no trade or education, but with a determination to make something of myself. The bars which were springing up everywhere to provide entertainment for the troops had taught me more of the outside world, if only I could escape from the confines of the village.

When I was released, I told my father I was going to England. My mother cried. My father was ashamed of the disgrace I had brought upon the family, and writing me off as a lost cause, paid my air fare. At last I would be able to enjoy life to the full, and my excitement grew as the departure day approached. My bragging to the other youths about what I would find abroad increased, even though most of it was conjecture on my part.

I arrived in England, barely able to speak English and knowing nothing about the country except the stories the soldiers had told me about the delights of London. I had assumed I would be welcomed in the bars of England in the same way as on my birth island. The reality was far different. It was cold, snowing and dismal when the plane landed, and the airport procedures were confusing. Somehow I made it through the immigration procedures, but the crowds and the frantic, impersonal atmosphere scared me. I had never seen so many people all in one place, but could not admit to feeling intimidated, even to myself.

Chapter Four

A distant cousin had married a miserable local girl and moved to London. Despite my inadequate English I managed to find a taxi to take me to the address scrawled on the piece of paper I had been given from home, although the fare made a large dent in my meagre funds. When I knocked on my cousin Joe's door, battered suitcase in hand, it was opened by his unsmiling, harridan of a wife. She had never liked me and the feeling was mutual, but I had no choice until I found my way around.

'Hello Katarina. I've come to see Joe,' I told her in our own language. 'Is he in?'

'He's at work. Where do you think he'd be at this time of the day?'

For a moment I thought she was going to shut the door in my face, leaving me destitute and abandoned in a strange city. My usual luck held out. It was only twenty minutes until her husband was due home so she begrudgingly let me in, and made me a cup of tea. Apart from that she scarcely spoke to me, but my relief when I heard the door open and my cousin came in was short-lived.

'What are you doing here? Have you escaped?'

'Only from narrow-minded people. I wanted to see London and thought you could put me up for a few days.'

The glare she gave him would have quelled a raging bull, but thankfully the tradition of hospitality won. Reluctantly they gave me a meal and a bed for the night. It wasn't quite the reception to the new, exciting, wild life I had expected, but at least I had somewhere to sleep. After a few days in the dingy flat with the sour-faced woman I was almost tempted to go home. From my narrow, single bed in the spare room their arguments went on well into the night, reverberating through the thin walls.

'How much longer is he staying? He does nothing but lounge around all day, stopping me getting on with the housework. And have you seen how much he eats? He's costing a fortune and not contributing a penny to help. The least he could do is get a job and pay some rent. You'll have to talk to him. I can't take much more. It's not as if he's pleasant company. Tell him he'll have to go.'

'He's alright really, just a bit young. We can't throw him out. What would people at home say if they found out? It would be unforgivable to leave him on his own. He doesn't even speak English but he'll learn. Just have a bit of patience. Now, how about a cuddle for your old man? It is my day off tomorrow.'

'You must be joking. With him around, listening? When I'm happy I'll think about making you happy. It's up to you.'

To get me out from under her feet, my cousin took me up to the West End of London, where he worked as a mini-cab driver. He left me to my own devices for the day, instructing me to meet him by Soho Square where he would pick me up at seven that evening. This was more like it. Wandering around Soho I was entranced by the glitter and the clubs. My eyes popped at the variety of goods in the shop windows, and the prices. Even at this time of day the restaurants were buzzing with people enjoying a meal. They put the swankiest places in the biggest towns at home to shame, and the exotic smells wafting from the kitchens reminded me it was nearly lunchtime. I didn't have the nerve or the funds to enter a café, but took the packet of sandwiches and bottle of Kinnie Katarina had given me into the small park. Sitting on a bench to people watch, the hazy sun did nothing to warm me up, but the length of the girls' skirts did. Some noticed me watching but turned away when they saw my cheap old-fashioned clothes, a few smiled then went on their way giggling.

The cold bit through me as I returned to the narrow streets where the buildings provided some protection from the icy wind. Had I been a fool to believe this new country held something for me? Returning to the club area, even though it was still daylight, the glamour proved I was right to have made my escape. Stopping outside a lurid window to gaze at the photos of semi-naked girls displayed in the showcases, I overheard my own language being spoken by a couple of bouncers standing just inside the doorway. Maybe because I was homesick I responded to a comment one of them made. Looking up in surprise they noticed me and replied. After that it was easy to move a few yards and join in their conversation. When I met up with my cousin a few hours later, I was bubbling with excitement.

'Hey Joe. Guess what? I've got myself a job. I start tomorrow, so you can give me a lift when you come in to work.'

Instead of being pleased, he gave me a suspicious look as if I had let him and our heritage down. Who needed losers like him and his wife? I had come to England to escape such pettiness, even if I never admitted to them the job at the club was sweeping up and cleaning tables from the debris of the night before. If asked, I hinted about working in a high-class West End London club; apart from that I kept my mouth shut. If everyone knew my business, I might as well have stayed at home delivering bread for my father. It was easier to give the impression of living the high life of my dreams, even though I was only on the perimeter.

Chapter Five

With money in my pocket and the longed-for freedom from family life, I settled into the routine, learning something new every day, but still wanted more. I didn't see the boss until the day he came in and called me over. Maybe he saw in me something of himself when he was my age.

'So, you're the kid they call TJ?' he said, looking me over. 'How do you like working here?'

'It's good, sir,' I responded, wondering what was coming next.

'You seem popular with the others, no one has complained about you and you do your job. Do you have any ambitions?'

How to answer? If I said no would he think I was settled, if I said yes, would he believe I was a trouble-maker?

'I like to learn,' I said, not knowing what else to say.

'How would you feel about doing night shifts? It's a lot different from the day work, but I think you'd be a good fit.'

Although I had no idea what was involved a smile crossed my face. 'Sure, that'd be good,' I told him, trying not to appear too eager.

When I turned up for work two days later the club looked totally different. During the day the mouldy wallpaper, dust and cobwebs were visible, but at night, with the lights dimmed and the place buzzing, it was all razzmatazz, gorgeous girls and life. On a good night, more money was thrust down a stripper's bra than I had paid for my horse. Champagne ordered by a group of toffs cost more than my father had hidden away.

As the weeks passed, I wondered what the guys at home would think of it all. Perhaps they would believe I was a film star if I turned up riding around the village in a limousine, wearing a smart Italian suit and proving they were the losers, not me. That was my dream. All I needed now was the money to make it come true. My wages were ten times as much as I had been paid at home, but it was nothing compared to the expense of living in London. My cousin had unenthusiastically rented me the spare room, and although at first it seemed a fortune, I soon realised the cost of major city existence.

I needed my own place to be able to come and go as I pleased, not have to sit through a prayer before meals, and put up with hand-wringing and wailing when I came in. Although they were early risers, without my own key I had to wake them up to let me in if it was a quiet night and my shift finished early, but the price of even the dingiest one room flat was way out of my reach. I carried on working at the club, listening and learning and keeping my eyes open and my mouth shut. The Swinging Sixties was when the boys ran Soho. I discovered why the club was never raided, and learnt the reason the local plods were given a drink on the house when they turned up, so they left smiling.

At work they discovered I was a great dancer, so in between sweeping floors I let loose to entertain the clients, and attracted the girls who hung out there. The tips were good but the attraction of a designer shirt, or a pair of soft Italian leather shoes was greater. My dress sense improved but my bank balance didn't. The bachelor pad stayed out of reach. There was no shortage of offers but even if I fancied a girl I had nowhere to take her. Then my life took a dramatic change.

Chapter Six

I was working as usual, chatting to the girls, running errands for the clients and pocketing the tips, when the boss turned up again. I hadn't seen him since the day he had put me onto the night shift but to my surprise he called me over to the bar.

'Hey, TJ. Come and join me for a drink. What're you having? Make it a large one, Tony and give me my usual.'

'Thank you, sir. Should I finish these floors first?'

'Do them later, for now come and have a chat.'

I ditched the mop and bucket and went to join him at the bar, half curious as to what was coming, and half proud to be invited. If it was bad news, surely he wouldn't be inviting me to join him. As I took a seat I wanted to look round and see who might be watching us having a drink together, as if we were friends and equals.

'Son,' he said, 'I been hearing about you.' My heart sank. Maybe this was it, no job, no money; perhaps I would be going home with my tail between my legs.

'You know how to keep your mouth shut, you do your job and you don't cause trouble. I need someone I can trust and think you could be my man.' I was so surprised I couldn't say a word, just looked at him. There was a moment or two of silence, then he laughed.

'That's what I mean, boy. Anyone else would be fawning and asking questions; you just hold your tongue and wait. I've got a special job for you if you're interested. It's a package I need delivered. You'll get cab fare but walk a bit and hail a taxi from somewhere else, not outside the club. When you get there, ask for Freddie. If he's not around, wait until he returns. If anyone asks just say Joe sent you. Then take the night off before you come back to the club. All clear?'

Removing my jacket, I put it on the chair between us. With a smile he acknowledged my move, and slipped a package into my pocket before he stood up and said goodnight. After he left, I wasn't sure what to do until the barman said "Your change," and thrust some money into my hand. I put it in my pocket without looking at it, but later saw it was more than enough for a trip right across London, plus a healthy tip for me.

'Your shift has finished for the night. Haven't you gone yet?' the club manager asked, which I took to mean the delivery should be done immediately. Following instructions, I walked for about fifteen minutes along the now familiar streets, then hailed a passing cab and thrust the piece of paper with the address under the driver's nose.

This was a new experience, but I sat back feeling special and trying to pretend I took cabs every day. I had learnt enough to make sure I left a tip, generous but not big enough for the cabby to remember me. He dropped me at a large warehouse building in the suburbs. It was dark and didn't have the buzz and bright lights of central London. For a moment I thought he had brought me to the wrong place, but when I rang the bell a bruiser of a guy opened the door straight away.

'Is Freddie in?' I asked tentatively.

'Who wants him?'

'Joe sent me,' I said.

The door opened and I was ushered inside. It looked like a film studio, with recording equipment, wires and cameras everywhere. Leading off the main area was a surprisingly homely room where a very short, bald man was watching TV. He turned it off as I came in, and greeting me with a toothless smile asked quietly, 'Hi. You got something for me?'

After confirming he was Freddie, I handed him the package which he put away without even glancing at it.

'Do you want a drink?'

'No thanks, I'm fine.'

'OK, I'll just sort you out some transport and you can get off.'

He made a call and less than a minute later a giant of a man with a distinctive scar on his face entered the room. Freddie said "Goodnight and thanks," and without a word the other guy led me to a car.

After driving for ten minutes he dropped me at a taxi rank and sped off, still without speaking. A cab drew up and I gave him my cousin's address. Usually I didn't get in until breakfast time, so I had the humiliation of having to knock on the door until my cousin woke and let me in. My mind was too full of the events of the evening to take in his muttered complaints about inconsiderate people disturbing his sleep.

In the privacy of my own room I counted what was left of the cash, and realised with a job like this once a week I would be able to afford my own place, and get out of this hell hole for good. Despite not having to work until the evening, the West End beckoned. I whiled away the time checking out the other bars and clubs and spending some of my hard-earned money, sure there would be plenty more where that came from. The next night it was down to earth with a bump as I went back to sweeping floors. Despite my lowly job I felt different, as if I belonged here and was one of the team. For a few days life went on as before; working at the club, collecting my tips and keeping my mouth shut. The boss didn't put in an appearance but one night the barman called me over and put a drink in front of me. I hadn't ordered one but he made it obvious I was to pay, so slightly puzzled, I handed over some cash.

  He came back with my "change," which was a lot more than he had been given in the first place. Putting it in my pocket I noticed a slip of paper giving an address. My reading had improved over the previous few months so I was able to work out the name of the area. Unsure what to do next as I hadn't been given a package, I was startled when the manager told me my shift was finished. He motioned towards my jacket which had a bag hanging over it, so I assumed this was the delivery. Walking away from the club before hailing a cab, curiosity got the better of me. Going into a cubicle in a public toilet I opened the bag and looked inside.

  Although it was fairly large, the sort of flight bag a businessman might use for an overnight stay, I had already noticed how light it was, so I wasn't surprised to find it was empty. A short walk located a taxi to take me to the address on the piece of paper. This time it was an old Victorian house in the suburbs, converted into bedsits, in a quiet road of similar houses. The number I wanted was the basement flat, which had its own front door along the side of the building, almost hidden by the overgrown garden. I might have missed it altogether if the door hadn't opened and a skinny, little man beckoned me inside. As he led me into the living room, I noticed through a partially open door another small room, again full of what looked to be recording and taping equipment.

'Help yourself to a whisky, or would you prefer something else?' the guy asked as he picked up the bag. 'I'll be back in a minute.'

I declined the whisky but accepted a coffee, thinking it would give me a chance to learn more about what was going on. He came back and handed me the bag which was a lot heavier than it had been before; in fact, I wondered how he had managed to carry it at all. Having finished my coffee, he directed me to the corner where I would be able to pick up a black cab to go back to the West End. The address for the delivery was one I knew; a seedy club where some of the girls earned some extra money stripping. I was to give the bag to someone called Paul, then go home and report for work as usual the following day.

I found a cab easily enough but my curiosity got the better of me and again I dodged into a public toilet to have a look at the contents. As expected, it was full of films with lurid covers and seductive women in poses that left little to the imagination. Hoisting the bag back onto my shoulder I felt something different under the cassettes. It wasn't a hard, plastic box like the others but a soft, well wrapped package, about six inches square. It would be obvious it had been tampered with if I tried to open it, and it was probably better if I didn't know what was inside. A short walk along the road brought me to the delivery address where I handed over the bag without problem.

When I went back to work the following evening it was as if nothing had happened. After two cab fares I didn't have much extra left from the "change" I had been given. Although I was disappointed it was better than nothing. My pay packet at the end of the week contained four times my normal wages; at this rate my own place could soon become a reality.

The pattern was set. Sometimes it was a collection, sometimes a delivery but always with a good bonus. I found myself a small flat in central London, my wardrobe of expensive suits grew as did the money in my pocket. I should have been happy realising my dreams, but the more I earned the more I spent, and the more I wanted. No longer the green country boy I had learnt how to eat at decent restaurants, how to act in sophisticated company - and how to gamble.

Chapter Seven

At first my usual good luck held but gradually losses overtook earnings, and I started gambling away my savings. I no longer swept floors but spent most of my shift collecting and delivering, before my life took another traumatic turn. I had made a pick-up and was hailing a cab when a car stopped and four hefty guys surrounded me. One flashed a badge; then I was bombarded with questions.

'Where have you been? What are you doing? Where are you going?'

I was scared but tried to brazen it out by replying 'What's it to you?' Before I knew it, I was bundled into the car and taken to the local police station. They kept me there all night, but I wouldn't budge from my story about arranging some films for a friend's stag night. The following morning they let me go, and surprisingly I was even allowed me to take the bag and its contents with me. Shattered but triumphant, I went home to wash and catch up with some sleep. On that occasion the bag only contained films and no flat packages, but later I discovered just how much fortune had smiled on me. If even two of the films had been the same, I could have been prosecuted for immoral material, but under the law, if they were all different, it could be claimed they were for personal use.

When I woke up I decided to go to the club early, hours before my normal night shift, and was reminded of how shabby it looked without the cover of subdued lighting. At that hour there were no customers, just a couple of cleaners and the barman checking his stock ready for the evening.

'The boss wants to see you,' he said as I walked in.

My heart sank. This was it, the end of my dreams. The barman took me through to a room at the back I'd never been in before. It had always been kept locked when I had been a cleaner, and I had been informed it was out of bounds. After knocking and hearing "Come in," Tony opened the door and ushered me through, closing it behind him to leave me alone facing the boss. He was sitting behind a huge, antique wooden desk, and as I stood there, he looked up and motioned me to come forward and take a seat. For a while there was silence as he looked through some paperwork and made some notes. Eventually he looked me straight in the eye.

'You did good son,' he said. 'Thought on your feet, kept your mouth shut and earned my respect. I believed in you and you didn't let me down. From now on, you're one of the team.'

I tried not to show my relief at his words, but at the same time knew that now was decision time. Was I in or out? I was in.

Chapter Eight

That was my life for the next few years, keeping my mouth shut, earning money, not asking questions, and ducking and diving when I got pulled in by the police. I learnt all there was to know about the clubs in Soho, the girls, the drugs, who to pay off and who to confront. Both the police and the council were regular visitors. You ignored the plebs and sucked up to the ones who could be useful, who would tip you off when a raid was due so you could show a semblance of respectability.

It was my busiest time, running out to the suburbs of London to hide the more explicit films, so we would appear small time, while allowing the law to bump up their target figures with petty arrests. It was a cat and mouse game and we all knew the rules. The phone call would arrive, the graphic material would be cleared and taken to a safe house, a few vanilla offerings would be left to be found during the raid, we'd pay a nominal fine, the stock would be returned to the club and life would continue as before. It was a team effort, but strangely, that's when I felt the loneliest and thought about the simple life at home. There I had been looked up to, not at the bottom of the ladder as I was here. Still, I had made my bed and had to lie in it. No way could I run back to my village as a failure.

    Perhaps because I was lonely, perhaps because the club girls no longer fawned over me and I had lost my novelty status, I hooked up with a woman from my own country. Although she had moved here with her parents when she was a youngster, she had been brought up the traditional way and accepted my word as law. Add to that the impression I gave of always having money to burn, and I appeared quite a catch. I wined and dined her for a few months and took her virginity. After a while she moved into my flat, and although it was good to have sex on tap, I might as well have been living at home with my family for all the freedom she gave me. If I was five minutes late she wanted to know where I had been, who I had seen, what I had been doing and what had happened to the housekeeping.

    Not surprisingly, when she discovered she was pregnant she wanted to get married. I ranted and raved a bit at her stupidity in not taking precautions, but it proved my manhood and I was excited at the thought of being a father. We had a quiet ceremony with her family and a few friends, although I didn't invite anyone from my working life. Bowing to tradition, I even agreed to a priest conducting the wedding in the local Catholic Church. At the reception afterwards I splashed out to prove my status; the champagne flowed like water and nobody could deny she had done well for herself.

Okay, maybe I shouldn't have come on quite so strong to one of the guests, but she was hot and sending me the signals. We were all drunk and my new wife shouldn't have tried to show me up in front of her friends. It wasn't an ideal wedding night after everyone left, but I had put a ring on her finger so she shouldn't have carried on like that. It was the first time I had to put her in her place; if you let them get away with it at the start you will never be a man in your own home. So what if she went off to sleep on the settee? I was too drunk to be up to much and at least I had some peace. She didn't apologise, but the next morning I came down to find a proper cooked English breakfast so I forgave her.

Marija and I bumbled along for a while, and she provided the services of a dutiful wife until it came nearer her time and she wouldn't let me touch her. Soon after my first child was born, I insisted on my conjugal rights and she fell pregnant again. I still worked hard in Soho, taking risks to put the best steak on the table to feed my growing family.

'You don't leave the table until you've eaten every scrap. Stop gagging and get on with it.'

'Greasy. Don't like fat.'

'Don't you dare give me cheek or you'll feel the back of my hand.'

'Leave him alone, TJ. He's only a baby.'

'He's not a baby, he's nearly four. I'm not wasting money on good food that doesn't get eaten. That's prime beef, not Spam. They should think themselves lucky. Have you any idea what that costs? They eat it or suffer the consequences. I'm off to work. Make sure he stays there until the plate's clean.'

As the boss of the family I demanded respect, especially from my wife. If she didn't understand, then a few slaps would soon put her straight. My father's ways had become my own. When she regained her figure, I insisted she went out and earned some extra money at one of the strip clubs. There was no point her lazing around while I worked my butt off, and she was a good-looking woman. She argued but I pulled a few strings and found her an afternoon job.

'It's not right, TJ. All those men gawping at me, and who would look after the children?'

'I will. You'll be home before I go to work and it's about time you earned your keep. It's not as if you keep me satisfied in bed, and anyway, the old blokes at that time of day couldn't get it up if they tried. You'll be safe enough and I promised Frank you'd start tomorrow.'

It worked out well. I was a good father, taking them to the park during the day to let off steam, and the sound of my raised voice was usually enough to keep them under control. If not, they would soon learn the hard way. I had enough to worry about as my gambling hadn't been paying dividends lately. The debts were piling up, and the people to whom I owed money were not the type to be patient. Still, she had no cause for complaint. There was food on the table for her and the kids. If she wanted a new dress from her earnings, she only had to ask. I looked after her pay packet but I never begrudged giving her the money to buy something nice to wear. Not cheap stuff though; if it wasn't designer it wasn't worth spending the cash. No way was my wife being seen in public wearing something that wasn't expensive.

I had moved a long way from being the scruffy country boy and she had to keep up my standards. It wasn't her place to know the risks I took just to keep things together. Eventually, with the pressure on me in the West End, I had to escape for a while until the heat died down. I told Marija I had some business to attend to, and if anyone asked, she was to say she didn't know where I was, or when I would be back, which was the truth. After she'd packed my best clothes I climbed into the Mercedes and headed for the coast. Outside London I felt more like the Jack-the-lad I had once been, before family pressures had taken over.

Chapter Nine

It was good to be free again. For a man on his own the girls were there for the taking, and not being known locally it was easier to join in with card games without my cheating reputation preceding me. At first, I threw a few games to install confidence in the yokels, but gradually discovered where the big play-offs took place. When the ships docked and the sailors hit the port town, they were only too ready to be parted from their wages, especially after a night spent drinking. Even if trouble brewed, I only needed to lie low for a few days and they would be back to sea, leaving the coast clear to take my chances with the next arrivals.

The night life was buzzing, not as seedy as its London counterpart, but with the same hierarchy and opportunities. My finances improved, and after a couple of months I was able to return home and pay off the Soho vultures.

'Where have you been? Weeks without a word and you swan back in like the dutiful husband returning from a hard day at work.'

It wasn't the greeting I expected, and the meal Marija was serving looked like shit after the high-class restaurants to which I had become accustomed.

'I wouldn't feed that to the pigs,' I yelled, throwing the plates against the wall. 'Get down to the butcher's before they close and buy something decent for dinner. Take this and don't be long. I'm hungry.' I thrust a ten-bob note into her hand, and by the time she returned the kids had finished their dinner, so I went to have a bath while she put them to bed and started frying the steaks. When I came down there was no sign of the broken crockery and a decent meal was waiting.

'You still working for Frank?' I asked as I finished off the final morsel.

'How else do you think I'd pay the bills?' Marija retorted. 'Once I've shelled out for someone to look after the children there's nothing left for fancy steak. We've been living on fresh air while you've been gallivanting.'

'Keep a civil tongue in your head,' I warned her. 'I'm back now so you can leave it to me. Get this lot cleared up then come to bed. I've had a long day.'

'You mean you're sleeping here tonight?'

'No, I've got a room at Buckingham Palace. Don't be stupid, woman. And make sure you get some food in for tomorrow. I'll see you upstairs. Don't be long.'

When she finally joined me in bed, she tried to pretend she was sleeping straight away, but I wasn't going to put up with her tricks. She was my wife, and it was her duty. The girls I'd had while I was away were just satisfying an urge, but this one wore my ring and had borne my kids. She kicked up a fuss at first, but the fight only made me more determined until eventually I was spent and able to roll over and sleep.

Chapter Ten

The following evening found me back at the club, unsure of the reception I would receive, or if they had found someone to take my place. It was a close-knit community and news travelled fast around Soho, but having been out of the area there was a chance I'd be able to bluff my way back in.

'Where ya been, TJ? We thought you'd run out on us, or been locked up.'

'My dad died suddenly, so I had to go home to sort things out,' I lied. Gambling provided a living but I needed some regular income. Whether the boss believed me or not he took me back, and the pick ups and deliveries became a regular thing again. For a while I kept my head down and only played low stakes games to pass the time. It was nothing compared to the big money pots of the past and frustration crept in. Things didn't improve at home. Marija cooked my meals and washed my clothes, but never showed any enthusiasm for love making. Typical woman. Once they'd got their claws into you, they were full of excuses.

'I'm tired, TJ. The kid's have been playing up. You stink of drink.'

The excuses changed but the outcome was the same. What had happened to the woman who had been only too eager to please me? Now every time turned into a fight but she had to learn. She had become such a cold fish it was hardly worth the effort, and my mind drifted back to the enthusiastic girls who had satisfied my needs while I was away. Then I'd had money to spare, but now she was forever whining about prices going up or the kids needing new shoes.

'You should go for the casinos, TJ,' Max said. I didn't know him very well but he had joined the game to make up the numbers, and I noticed him watching me while we played. I think he probably broke even but the other two lost. You'd think it was a fortune the way they carried on, and I ended up throwing my winnings on the table in disgust. After playing all night there was scarcely enough to pay for a decent meal.

'You're crazy,' I told him. 'The businesses know what they're doing, not like these pussies who panic if they lose a few quid. The odds are stacked against the punters, and I wouldn't want to take my chances against the Chinks. They can be mean bastards when they all stick together.'

'No, not them. It's not worth the risk. I mean the casinos themselves. We could team up and split the profits.'

'What profits? No one gets that lucky playing it straight.'

'Who said anything about straight? The guy I used to work with has gone home and I need a new partner. But not round here. We're too well known.'

The first time we hit a small out-of-town casino I was shit scared. Max had given his instructions and was full of confidence. We were to pretend not to know each other, but work in tandem. I was to keep an eye out for security while losing steadily, and kick up a bit of a fuss to distract attention. At that time there were very few cameras and he showed me who to look out for. After a few hours I caught his signal and once he left, gave him five minutes then followed to where we had left the car. The amount I'd lost wasn't much but it was enough to put me in a bad mood.

When he climbed into the passenger's seat, I was too annoyed to speak to him until he told me to pull off into a lay-by.

'What's the point of stopping?' I asked. 'It's been a waste of time and I want to get home.'

He turned to me and grinned as he threw a fist full of large denomination notes into my lap. 'Here you go. That's your share. Fifty-fifty like I promised. Next time I'll be the patsy and you do the winning.'

It became a regular arrangement but we had to change the venue frequently so we didn't get rumbled, and there were only so many gambling dens within easy reach. Although I now had two regular incomes it still wasn't enough. Occasionally we travelled down to my old haunts at the coast, but that meant I wasn't around for the deliveries. It wouldn't be wise to piss off the owner of the club but there was no way I could be in two places at once.

Chapter Eleven

For a while we ran up and down, my Mercedes car eating up the miles as we travelled between London and the coast, building up our reserves for bigger and better games. I was hardly ever at home, only using it as a base for eating, sleeping and changing my clothes. Now the boys were growing up my wife had put the youngest in with his brother, and moved her clothes into the spare room. leaving the main bedroom for me. Occasionally I demanded my rights, but most of the time it was good to have space for myself without her constant nagging. After all, I was working myself stupid to earn some money for a better life, and I allowed her to keep the cash she earned from stripping when I was away.

As for my other needs, well, there were plenty of girls only too eager when Max and I pulled an overnighter. After one particularly crazy night in Portsmouth, when we had won big and several girls from the casino joined us to celebrate, it crossed my mind how free women had become with their favours.

'You don't need those, TJ. I'm on the pill. We can have some fun without worrying now. This is the 60s, not the dark ages.'

At first, I was reassured when the slut made it clear there was no thought of long-term commitment. The last thing I needed was a one night stand I hardly knew, chasing me for support if she fell for a sprog. If she went with me, she'd as likely go with others, and this one had already told me she was married. Her husband was an older guy who kept her in a grand house, but thought Christmas and birthdays were enough to keep a ravishing, thirty-something satisfied. Although I knew my own wife wouldn't dare go out on the town with her friends like this one, it made me think. There were plenty of saddos at the club where she still worked. If they were getting enough, they wouldn't have been there bringing in her wages, and no way was I going to be a patsy for someone else's kid.

'TJ, is that you?' Marija called when I returned home the following morning.

'Who were you expecting? Your fancy man? It's about time you got yourself on the pill. Make yourself an appointment at the doctors tomorrow. While I'm away slaving for you, I don't want to come home and find there's another mouth to feed because you've been careless.'

'When would I have the chance to find someone else? If I'm not working, I'm with the kids. You know I've never looked at another man. Why are you so cruel? We were married in church and I respect our marriage vows, even if you don't.'

'What do you mean by that?'

I was tired, exhausted from the pressure of living on my nerves at the casinos, and that was the thanks I got. My so-called loving wife was giving me cheek as soon as I stepped in the door. How did I know she hadn't been shagging the clients at work while I was trying to earn a living out of town? There was only one way to find out.

'No, TJ. I've only just got the kids off to school. The weekend is always busy at the club and I need to catch up on some sleep.'

Well! If that wasn't proof she had been playing around while I was away, I don't know what was. If she could spread her legs for the punters, she sure as hell could for her husband. Later she could get herself sorted but for now I intended to take what was due to me, whether she liked it or not.

When I woke up the house was quiet, and I realised she had probably gone off to work. So much for being a proper wife. If I wanted something to eat, I'd have to make it myself, or go out to a café somewhere. My father wouldn't have stood for it and neither would I. Things had to change. Never mind we were in a more enlightened country, some traditions needed to be preserved.

'Papa, you're home.' My two boys rushed up to throw their arms around me and give me a hug. 'We drew pictures at school and teacher said mine was good. Look, Papa. Look.'

I took the piece of paper my eldest thrust at me, which looked like a blob with curly hair wearing a skirt, accompanied by two smaller blobs. There was no man in the picture.

A teenager followed the boys in, looking surprised at finding someone in the house.

'Hi, you must be TJ. I'm Jackie. I pick the kids up when Marija is working. She told me you were in the navy so I guess you've got some leave. Nice to meet you.'

I didn't know what to say but played along. After all, she was an attractive young piece, but I would have words with my wife later. How dare she make up stories about me without giving me warning? Was she trying to make me look stupid?

'Hello, Jackie. Thanks for helping with the children. I keep telling my wife she should be looking after them but she likes to be the boss. You know what it's like. Or perhaps you've not married?'

'No, I'm on my own. Not even a steady boyfriend.'

'What? A beautiful girl like you? The men around here must be blind. Have you got time for a cuppa?'

'I usually give the boys their tea then read them a story until Marija comes home, but if you're here I don't suppose you need me,' she replied.

'Don't say that,' I smiled at her. 'I definitely need you. To make something for the kids, I mean.' When I winked, she giggled. With the boys around I'd no opportunity to take things further, but from the look she gave me I knew it was only a matter of time. Watching her reaching up to the top shelf, the glimpse of stockings under her mini had my libido raging. The little tart was teasing me and if it hadn't been for my wife coming in at that moment, I might have forgotten the boys and given her what she was asking for.

'TJ, are you still here? Oh, hello Jackie. I hope they haven't been any trouble.'

'Good as gold, Marija. You've got a lovely family.' Although it was an innocent comment, my wife's face looked like thunder as she caught the glance Jackie gave me. 'Yes, well, I'll be off then. See you tomorrow.'

'Don't bother to pick them up tomorrow, Jackie,' Marija said through tight lips. 'If TJ's not here I'll take an afternoon off and do it myself.'

'Oh, OK then. Bye.' This time Jackie kept her heard down as she quietly closed the door behind her.

'What do you mean you'll take time off?' I rounded on my wife before she could start nagging. 'And what's all this about me being in the navy? You trying to take the piss?'

'You might as well be in the navy for all we see of you,' she retorted. 'What should I tell people? That you're a loving caring father working in a proper job? Or admit you're a cheating jerk who thinks he's God's gift?'

Frustration and anger bubbled inside me, and my arm lashed out, catching her square across the face.

'Don't you dare speak to me like that, you cheap slut. You're the one taking your clothes off in some cheap dive, instead of being here looking after my children like a proper mother. You make me sick. I should never have let you trick me into putting a ring on your finger. And sort those snivelling brats out. I'm going to work.'

My mood didn't improve when I entered the club and the boss had no deliveries or collections lined up for me.

'Sorry, TJ. The plods have been on our case and we need to lie low for a bit. Perhaps you could help the lad with some cleaning. He's willing, but not got much idea.'

Is this what I'd come down to? Teaching a snotty-nosed teenager how to mop out the bogs? Stuff them all. At the bar Tony pushed a large one in my direction.

'Here you go, TJ. You look like you need it. On the house.'

'Thanks, Tony,' I said knocking it back in one gulp. 'So, what's been going on while I was away? What's all this about the coppers coming on strong?'

'Our snitch on the council got the sack when they discovered he'd been on the take. The bastard didn't even tell us, so when the law turned up, we were caught with our pants down, as it were. Luckily there wasn't too much heavy stuff on the premises but the boss wasn't a happy bunny. There's talk of a court case and a serious fine. It's not surprising he's turned into Snow White until the heat dies down. If you've got another option, I'd make the most of it for a while. Leave me a contact number and I'll give you a bell when things are back to normal.'

'Cheers, Tony. You're a good bloke. I'll see you right when the time comes. Tell the boss I'm taking some time off for a while. '*Sahha u Grazie.*' Goodbye and thanks.

At least now I could concentrate on the job which was bringing in the most money, without worrying about having to keep in with Soho. Other nationalities were staring to muscle in and it was time to move on. The times they were a changing.

Chapter Twelve

Max had no commitments and was only too pleased to get out of London, so the following morning saw us heading back to the coast where I felt more at home. As we intended staying for a while, we needed a place to live. He knew a guy from the old country and we took rooms in one of the houses he owned and let out. Rents here were much lower than in the city, we could come and go as we pleased and life was sweet. As we gained experience in working as a team, the wad under my mattress grew and we became professional gamblers, travelling all over the south of England as we discovered new spots to hit.

For a while life was good. The money was coming in regularly, the girls were hot, and I had no sour faced woman or screaming off-spring to cramp my style. Even if it didn't have the London style, I wasn't looking over my shoulder every minute, or waiting for the next raid. It was a slower pace of life but there was plenty of action, and even if the locals called me wild, they showed me respect.

'Hey, TJ.' Charlie called out to me when he saw me in town one evening. 'There's a new club just opened up. I hear they've got a fab band. You fancy coming along? It wouldn't be the same without you showing off your moves.'

'You think you're the *News of the World*? Tell me something I don't already know. You forget who you're talking to, mate. I've got some business to sort first but I'll be there. Keep the birds sweet until I arrive.'

'Sure thing, TJ. See you later.'

Charlie was a little runt of a guy with a spotty face, and too shy to chat up women on his own. I don't know why I let him hang around with me, but he had a good nature, and could never be classed as competition when I was on the pull. If there were a couple of girls out together it was not unusual for me to end up with both, and I was man enough to handle it. Max and I had arranged to hit some casinos, but they were fairly close and we should be back in time for when the night-spot was nicely warmed up. Fate was shining on us that night, and we cleaned up big time. With a thick wad in my pocket I was buzzing when we hit the club, the music was great and with several brandies fuelling my blood, the timing was perfect to let rip and party. Which I did with a vengeance.

The eyes of nearly every woman in the place followed my gyrating hips as I owned the dance floor, although the cash in my pocket dwindled as I bought round after round of drinks. Who cared? There was plenty more where that came from, and the adulation was food for my long-forgotten, country boy soul. I'd spotted the beautiful blue-eyed, blonde sitting with her friends, but although she smiled when I caught her eye, some bimbo dragged me off to dance and when I looked back, she was gone.

That was a night to remember, even if the mega hangover the next day made me tired and grumpy. My mood didn't improve when I checked my stash and found there was precious little left from our exceptional winning streak. Most of it had been blown on the good-time girls, but when my brain cleared, there was only one woman on my mind. I tried the disco a few more times that week but the atmosphere wasn't the same, and she wasn't there. Even our run of luck at the casinos turned. At the weekends they were busy and it was easier to remain incognito and make the odds work in our favour. During the week there were fewer punters and we nearly got caught when a pit boss noticed Max slipping me a winning card. We blustered our way out, insisting we didn't know each other, but although they didn't call the fuzz, we were both banned. Not a good sign as it restricted our opportunities and word could get round to the other casinos in the area.

Quite by chance I stopped at a café in a town some miles from my digs. Max was due to meet me at the local casino later in the evening but I had arrived early, and didn't fancy a pint as I needed to keep my wits about me. Things had become even more difficult, and more often than not we only managed to break-even. I was contemplating giving it up and heading back to London, and then I saw her- my beautiful English rose. She was sitting on her own at a corner table, a posh looking carrier bag on the floor next to her.

'Hi,' I said. 'Remember me? From the club a few weeks ago.'

She looked up and smiled as I sat down. 'Hello, TJ. I didn't expect to see you around here.'

'You know my name, but I don't know yours. What do they call you?' I asked, pleased that she had been interested enough to find out who I was.

'Sarah,' she grinned, holding out her hand to shake mine. 'Pleased to meet you officially.'

'Nice to meet you too, Sarah. I looked for you to have a dance but you'd disappeared.'

She gave me that beautiful smile again. 'I was with some friends but my father insisted on picking us up. He doesn't like me to stay out late, and it was difficult enough to get his permission to go in the first place. He means well, so I don't want to upset him. Anyway, you looked as if you had plenty of ladies only too willing to dance with you.'

'But it was you I really wanted. Do you like dancing? And how did you know my name?'

'My friend overheard someone calling you. And yes, I love it. Do you always dance like that? Or was it the drink making you so wild?'

'Come out with me one night and I'll show you I can do slow dances too. How about Tuesday? I could pick you up. What's your address?'

'Whoa, slow down a bit. I've only just met you, and somehow I don't think my dad would approve. He's a bit old-fashioned like that.'

'What's it got to do with him? You're old enough to do as you like.'

'Not really. I'm only sixteen. How old are you.'

'Twenty-three,' I lied. It wouldn't do to put her off if I admitted my real age, and she might start to wonder if there was a wife hidden somewhere in the background. It was likely she was still a virgin but I wanted her, more than I'd ever wanted a woman before.

'Well, I'd better be getting home,' she said as she collected her bags and stood up. 'It was nice seeing you again, TJ.'

'I've got the car outside. Let me drop you.'

'It's not a problem, I can catch the bus. It's not far.'

'No way. Come on. I'll give you a lift,' I said, all thoughts of having a coffee long forgotten. We'd only been driving a few minutes when she indicated for me to pull over. It was a nice area, with large expensive houses and I was impressed.

'Which one is yours?' I asked as I brought the car to a halt.

'Actually, I live in the next road, but I don't want my family to see you dropping me off. You can't imagine the third degree they'd give me if they saw a strange man driving me home.'

'But when will I see you again? I've got some business tonight but I could change it if you'd agree to come out with me.'

'I can't tonight. It's my sister's birthday. That's why I was out shopping for a new dress for her party. I could meet you Tuesday lunchtime, in the café where we were today. That's my day off. Oh, I just thought. You'll probably be working.'

'No, that's OK. Most of my work is at night. I'll see you there. Tuesday, about twelve. Don't let me down.'

'I won't. Thanks for the lift,' she said as she got out of the car, looking back to blow me a kiss as she turned the corner.

It seemed she was my lucky charm as that night our luck turned, and once again Max and I cleaned up at the casino. She turned up for our date as promised, and that was the start of the next episode in my life. Sarah was everything I had ever dreamt of; classy, well-bred, and from a good old-fashioned English family. Under normal circumstances she was way out of my normal sphere of contacts, but somehow fate had played into my hands, and we began to meet regularly. I told her I owned a night-club, which made our meetings during the afternoons and evenings easier for her to explain away, as I was able to drop her home at an hour early enough to keep her father happy.

Underneath her naïve innocence, her passionate response to my kisses showed me she was all woman, but she would never come back to my place so I could finish what we started. It was probably just as well, as my dingy room was a far cry from the luxurious home to which she was accustomed. It reminded me of those long-ago days when I had lodged with my cousin. I took my satisfaction elsewhere and longed for the day when I could show her the real meaning of sexual love.

Chapter Thirteen

'Oh God. It's my Dad.'

After a few months during which she allowed me more access to her beautiful body, I was dropping her home when a tall, distinguished man walked past the car. Although she turned her face to sit demurely in the passenger seat, I knew he had seen us.

'I'll come in with you. It's about time I met your family.'

'No, TJ. Not yet. Let me deal with it first. Once I've explained and he's calmed down you can come over for tea and meet them properly. Give me time to tell them about you first. It will be easier that way. He still thinks of me as his baby, but I'll bring him round. I'll see you Tuesday as usual.'

She was very quiet when we met on our usual date, but asked if instead of meeting in the café the following week, I would like to come to her house. I was nervous but determined to make a good impression. At the appointed hour I turned up, dressed in a smart suit and carrying an enormous bunch of flowers which I presented to her mother as she opened the door to greet me. It was obvious where Sarah got her looks from. The older woman exuded sex appeal and if I hadn't been besotted with Sarah, I would definitely have made a play for her.

'TJ. They're beautiful Thank you so much. Do come in and meet my husband. We've heard so much about you.'

It was an encouraging start but the reception from Sarah's father was distinctly more frosty. Over tea and polite conversation, I learnt he had been a navy officer so was well aware of the reputation of my fellow countrymen. He was now a successful architect, working on the reconstruction of the many buildings still recovering from the devastation of the war years. His questions as to my prospects and intentions were awkward, but I tried to reassure him by saying I was building up my future by investing in the entertainment industry. In an effort to appease his suspicions I asked his advice on property purchases in the area, and by the time I took my leave, was confident he would accept me as his daughter's boyfriend. Sarah was very subdued and hardly said a word, in contrast to her mother who was definitely sending out the signals. Thanking them for their hospitality I was pleased to make my escape.

Despite my conflicting emotions Max and I won big that night, and with decent money in my pocket I determined to show Sarah's parents I was good enough for their daughter, even if I knew her family didn't approve of me. Maybe they saw me for what I was - a simple country foreigner who made money from things they would never discuss in polite society. Sarah was young and naïve but I was sure I could win her over. There were still plenty of women fawning over me but I wanted the best.

The first day we made love in my sordid bedsit, I realised I had taken her virginity. She was only sixteen but was a fast learner and having tasted, I wanted more. Despite the wife and children I had in London, I convinced her we would be married soon, and everything would work out once her family accepted us. A second invitation to tea with her parents wasn't forthcoming, but she started spending more and more time at my digs. It was about two months later when she turned up at my door, suitcase in hand and tears streaming down her face.

'TJ, I've left home. Dad wouldn't listen and we had a blazing row. Even Mum wouldn't stick up for me. He said I've got to stop seeing you. It's not fair. Can I stay with you tonight?'

As it happened, I'd nothing arranged for work that evening, so I dried her tears and took her to bed to comfort her. It was good to have her available, but after my first mistake I wasn't sure about having another woman around full-time. The following day I dropped her home, telling her to let her parents know she was safe, and I'm meet her Tuesday as usual. At the café she was unresponsive, only saying her father had been worried about her and on the verge of calling the police. Thankfully he didn't know where I lived, and although she had returned home, she continued to spend most weekends sleeping in my bed. It was a quiet time for the casinos, and I was ashamed when looking at my grubby hovel compared with the beautiful house where she had been brought up.

'Money's not important, TJ,' she told me. 'I don't care about all that, you're all I want.'

Chapter Fourteen

After another row at home she moved in, and committed herself to me totally, believing my story about being the owner of a successful London club. It was easy to convince her my cashflow was a temporary problem as a reaction to the enthusiastic rises in living standards of the past few years. The news backed up my assertions, and despite her far superior education she trusted me as her mentor. Max and I still went out working the gambling dens, but they were becoming few and far between and I needed a new source of income.

'TJ, I've been thinking,' she told me when I arrived home after a particularly bad night. Never a good phrase to greet a man on a losing streak, who only wanted a bath, food, sex and sleep without listening to a woman's complaints.

'It's not fair you work so hard and I sit around all day doing nothing. I could go out and get a job, help out for a bit to bring in some money.'

'What? You think I'm not man enough to keep my woman? What do you take me for? You trying to make me a laughing stock?' My frustrations bubbled over and she looked quite shocked, never having seen me in a temper before.

'No, of course not. Don't be mad at me, I only want to help and see you happy again. There must be something I can do.'

'Sorry, babe. It's been a hard week. Come to bed and cheer me up.'

It started me thinking. She was pure and innocent, and ripe to be taught the ways of the world when there was so much money to be made. The respectable judges, bank managers and more upmarket members of society here at the coast were a far cry from the drunken louts of the West End, but they had the same needs. The elite of the local community needed gratification from a beautiful woman, before going back to their expensive homes and ugly wives, and I was in a position to supply the goods.

'There's nothing to worry about,' I told her. 'I'll be there to look after you. You just need to be nice to him. He's an important client. Just turn on the charm and flirt a bit. You'll be wonderful and he'll be happy which will be good for business.'

She wasn't convinced, but did as she was told. We had dinner at an expensive restaurant, and although she flinched when his hand strayed to her knee under the table, she kept her cool and didn't rock the boat.

'She's a gorgeous piece, TJ,' the guy said when we were alone. 'And fresh, not like some of the old bags round here. Is she on offer?'

'Sorry, mate, you couldn't afford her,' I teased. 'But give it time. Who knows? I'll keep you in mind when she's ready.'

It gave me food for thought. Yes, she was my woman but her youth, breeding and looks made her worth a fortune. Had fate played into my hands? Over time I built up the clientele and she provided the service. She didn't like the life but loved me, and had learnt to do what she was told. The first time I let a guy have more than a grope she was distraught, and it took a lot of effort not to rush in from the next room and play the outraged boyfriend. Still, the money he paid me gave me the strength to wait a while until he collapsed, satisfied.

'Where were you, TJ? Do you know what he tried to do to me? I was scared and you weren't there when I needed your help,' she sobbed.

'Sorry, babe. I went out for some cigarettes. I'll have a word with him. We won't see him again. Let me give you a cuddle. You'll feel better tomorrow. You know I love you.'

To please her I changed tactics. Instead of full sex I realised there was more money to be made in the kinky stuff. Any man would get hard at the sight of her in high heels and black basque. The whip in her hand was the icing on the cake. Surprisingly, considering her upbringing, she had a natural instinct for the work, or perhaps she felt it less invasive. Either way, it was productive and a welcome change from the constant stress of being caught cheating in the casinos. The bank balance grew healthy again.

For a while, things were fine but one night, after a particularly busy week with clients, she turned away when I put my arms around her, ready for some personal action. Although I used all the tricks to get her going, her heart wasn't really in it, and I was only partially satisfied. Rolling over, I lit a cigarette while I waited for her to come back from the bathroom.

'What was that all about?' I asked, as she returned to bed but kept her distance.

'TJ, I need to talk to you,' she said quietly. 'This isn't the life I expected. I gave up my family thinking it would be just you and me, but now….'

'Why is everything about you,' I turned on her, 'after all I've done for you. How easy do you think it is to set up the contacts and demean myself, just to bring in the business. All you have to do is flounce around a bit. I'm the one working non-stop to bring in the money. And then you can't even keep me satisfied when we're in bed. Would you rather go back to giving it away? You make me sick. How long do you think you'd survive without me around to protect you? You'd end up like those scrubbers up against a tree for a few bob, instead of having me protecting you and looking after you properly.'

My voice came out louder and angrier than I intended. Maybe it was because I hadn't received the enthusiastic response, which had been her usual reaction to our love making when we first met. Perhaps I was scared about losing my main source of income. If I pushed too hard she might walk, but if I was too soft, she would never show me respect.

'I'm sorry, TJ. Don't be angry with me. I miss my family and they want me to visit them.'

'What makes you think that? Who have you been talking to?'

'I bumped into a neighbour today and she told me.'

'So now you're gossiping about our private business to everyone? Why don't you just take out an advert in the News of the World? As if I haven't got enough to worry about without you blathering to all and sundry. Run on back like the spoilt little brat you are. You'll be doing me a favour. Now let me get some sleep.'

I was taking a chance but life was a gamble. If she wasn't committed enough there were plenty more where she came from. When I woke the next morning there was a full English breakfast waiting for me, and although her eyes were puffy, she still looked classy. It would be a shame to lose her.

'Is the coffee hot enough, TJ? Would you like some more bacon? I'm sorry about last night. I won't mention it again.'

'It's fine. Listen, if you really want to go and see your parents you can go tomorrow. But don't expect me to go with you. And no telling them all my business. Just say "Hello," and make sure you come back to me, OK?'

'Oh, TJ, Thank you. I love you. I promise I won't stay more than an hour. I'll be back before you get home. You won't even know I've gone.'

The smile lighting up Sarah's face made it worthwhile to give in to her, and she became the loving woman she used to be. Our sex life was good, she worked hard with the clients, and perhaps she had grown up from the little girl she used to be. I let her visit her parents now and again, but put my foot down when it started to get too frequent. Once every couple of months was enough. No point in letting her have too much freedom to spread rumours and bring me grief.

Chapter Fifteen

It was her idea to open a joint safe deposit box at the bank. There were plenty of villains about, and it wasn't good to have too much cash lying around, especially if the police should happen to visit, and start wondering where it came from. I didn't like the idea of all the nosey bank staff seeing what was in an account, but as Sarah explained, this was private and they had no access. I was the only one with a key. She found us a decent flat in a good part of town with a reasonable rent, and took delight in turning it into a good home. Sarah had excellent tastes and it was a far cry from the peasant hovel I had been brought up in. With money rolling in life was good.

Times were changing. The original upper crust clientele became harder to find and sex was everywhere, free of charge. I despised the way the pureness of the English breed was being infiltrated, with foreigners flooding the country, mixing their blood and destroying the traditional beauty of the English women. It took an exorbitant price before I would accept one as a client for her, and even then, I stood guard in case they tried to get more than their money's worth.

From a baker's delivery boy, I had now become a bodyguard, but a rich one.

I rarely went back to London, but somehow my wife found out my new address. Even far from home my countrymen loved to tittle-tattle and with everyone someone's cousin, it wasn't too difficult to track me down. With the grapevine working overtime I told Sarah I had to attend to some business at my London club and drove back to see Marija. The welcome I received from my wife wasn't what a man deserved. Even the kids looked at me as if I was a stranger. Anyone would think I'd been away for years, but they had grown so much in those few short months. I had brought presents for the children and thrust some money in my wife's hand, but she got angry and blamed me for deserting her and leaving her struggling, after all she had given up for me. When I asked her how much she wanted to get off my back she went crazy. Women! You give them everything and still they're not satisfied.

After a few days I'd had enough. She wouldn't give me my dues as her husband, and her narrow-minded mentality reminded me of the cold peasant my cousin had married. At least I could escape to the loving welcome of my sophisticated English lady. I stuck it out for a week, then high-tailed it back to the coast. There was nothing much left for me in London, and I needed to get back to protect my investment. The welcome I received from Sarah when I returned was everything a man could ask for.

'TJ. I've missed you. How did the business trip go? Did you get everything sorted out? If I'd known you were coming home tonight, I'd have cooked you something special. All I've done is rattle around in the flat all day. Sorry, but I couldn't work without you around to protect me, and anyway no one has asked for me. It's good to have you home.'

'Wow. Slow down woman,' I said, trying to hide my delight that she was beginning to realise how much she needed me. 'I ate before I left, but I'm hungry for you. We'll both have a night off and relax a bit. Now, come to bed and show me how much you've missed me. I'll get some work sorted for you tomorrow.'

That was as it should be; a proper reception and a willing woman. When I woke the next morning, a hot breakfast was waiting, and after visiting a few contacts I had appointments lined up for the following few days. Word was getting around about the availability of class, and due to her upbringing, she was accepted in the best five star hotels without question. Sarah was a stunning woman and totally at home in the refined establishments. Despite my designer clothes, the trumped-up receptionists sometimes looked twice at me, however much money I threw around. She turned on the charm and we seldom had a problem when meeting clients.

'No, TJ, leave it to me. Don't make a fuss,' she whispered to me on one occasion when a particularly snotty little office boy challenged us when we were taking a lift up to a designated assignment in a luxury suite.

I wanted to punch the little shit, but stayed back as she went up to the desk. He glanced in my direction several times, until she leaned forwards and he got an eyeful of her assets in her low-cut cocktail dress.

'We're sorted. Let's not keep him waiting,' she told me as she pressed the button for the top floor accommodation.

'The little runt. You should have let me teach him to keep his eyes to himself. What did you say to him?'

'Calm down, TJ. He's only doing his job. I told him we had a business appointment with a client, and you were there as my bodyguard. For the clientele who stay in this type of hotel that's quite common, especially for a woman on her own.'

'You should have told him I was your man. I've a good mind to go and put him straight.'

'Leave it, TJ, please. 342. This is it,' she said as she knocked on the door.

'You must be Christina. Reception told me you were on your way up. And this gentleman is?'

'A lady should never travel alone, Mr Christos. Have you somewhere he could wait while we conduct our business?'

'Call me George, my dear. Of course. Perhaps your friend would like to watch TV in the sitting area, while we adjourn to my private room. Please help yourself to some coffee, young man. This way, Christina, I have some champagne on ice waiting.'

All my negotiations had been arranged through various flunkies, so I had never actually met this man before. Now I was dismissed as if I was a lowly servant, but they had paid a big deposit upfront, and I trusted Sarah to collect the rest of the money due, before coming up with the goods. What was with all this "Christina?" Her name was Sarah, but perhaps she was right to call herself something else, so she would be less traceable. It was annoying I hadn't thought of it first, but that didn't stop me seething as I sat on the luxurious settee to watch some boring programmes.

With the sound down low, at first I could only hear the sounds of muted conversation, but after a while I heard a deep voice groaning in ecstasy. I felt my own libido rising and was tempted to join them. Just as it became too much to bear, Sarah came out of the room and beckoned me to follow her, putting her fingers to her lips to keep me from saying anything.

'That was wonderful, I'll be sure to contact you when I'm next back on business.

Thank you, Christina. l look forward to seeing you again,' the guy said as he came out of the bedroom, wearing only the hotel supplied gown.

Sarah looked flushed but composed as we took the lift back to the ground floor in silence. What I had to say could wait until we were alone. I pushed through the swing doors without bothering to wait for her, but noticing she wasn't behind me, turned to see her talking to the young creep at reception. By the time the taxi dropped us home my blood was boiling.

'I thought you were something,' I told her as we prepared for bed. 'What was all that with the kid at the hotel? For God's sake he was nothing. You need to learn where the money is, not chat up some pimply youth who's probably never had it.'

'TJ. If this is going to get us a better life you need to learn how things work. He could get us banned from the hotel so I needed to keep him sweet. George was a good client. He told me he always stays at that hotel, and he gave me a very generous tip. Here, make sure you go to the bank tomorrow, and put this in the box.'

The money she threw at me was a lot more than the final fee I was expecting. Perhaps she was right, but I still didn't like being treated as the hired help. I was the boss and I deserved respect from my women; it wasn't right for them to think they were in charge. Sarah was good at the job though, and many of the clients became regular customers. The money rolled in and the safe deposit box was bursting. There was no problem with the local fuzz; the odd freebie for a high court judge, or senior police inspector saw to that.

Chapter Sixteen

The problem came from an unexpected quarter. Returning home one afternoon I was confronted by a cosy scene in the living room- my wife sitting on the settee drinking tea with Sarah.

'What the hell is going on?' I yelled, shaken at the sight of Marija, and wondering how much she had said. How dare she come here to track me down. Switching to our native language I turned on her.

'Why are you here? Who told you where to find me? What lies have you been telling? Are you crazy?' I was blustering but I had too much to lose if she rocked the boat with Sarah. It had taken me a lot of hard work to get to this position, and I couldn't afford to let some jealous bitch destroy it.

'I knew it,' Marija sobbed, turning on the water works. 'You'll never change. I didn't want to believe them but I should have known you'd be shacked up with some woman.'

'I asked you a question,' I shouted over her whining. 'Which bastard has been shooting his mouth off? Tell me before I have to beat it out of you.'

'What are you saying?' Sarah asked, looking at first me, then Marija. 'Please speak English. I want to know what's going on. This lady had only just arrived when you came in, TJ. She says she knows you from London. Why are you so angry?'

'Shut it or you'll regret it.' I spoke before my wife had a chance to say anything more, then switched back to English. 'Sorry, Sarah. I forgot you don't understand our language. Marija, I'll give you a lift back to the station.'

The look I gave my wife was enough to quell any further arguments, and I grabbed her arm and forced her out of the door before she could say anything more than goodbye to Sarah. In the car I insisted she told me what she had said, and which scumbag had been opening his mouth so I could sort him out. Why was I not surprised when she told me it was Katarina, my cousin's wife who had stirred things up? That bitch had always hated me and this was her way of paying me back, after I had given her money all the time I lived in her miserable hovel. It seemed Katarina had got into the habit of dropping in to see Marija, and with nothing better to occupy their narrow minds, my wife had started bleating about how long it had been since she had seen me.

    I could imagine her haranguing Joe until he asked around and the grapevine found my address. Even living in another country it was still a close-knit community, and the small-mindedness was not restricted by seas and oceans. Joe was as much of an old woman as those two. He should have kept his wife in order, not acted like a pussy and encouraged them. At least Marija confirmed she had only just arrived when I turned up. Although she now knew where I lived, she hadn't had an opportunity to say anything more. For all Sarah knew, she could be a distant cousin or married to someone else. That was the way it was going to stay. Thrusting some money into Marija's hand, I made sure she caught the train. When she started grumbling about needing to talk to me, I promised her I'd come to see her in London within a week or two to sort things out. Now all I had to do was convince Sarah the only thing I had shared with Marija was our country of birth.

Chapter Seventeen

The storm blew over, but although I managed to convince Sarah her visitor was just a spiteful friend of my cousin's wife, she still seemed suspicious. It was only when I told her Marija had taken a shine to me and been upset when I rejected her, that she started to believe me. True to my word, I made a trip to London to find out what had inspired the visit. Typically, it seemed to be all about money.

'TJ. You've no idea how difficult it was to bring up the children without any support. The childminders are so expensive, but I've got to work. How else can I make some money to feed and clothe them? It's so difficult on my own. You seem to be doing alright. They're your children too.'

She must have heard I'd had moved on to a better life and wanted a slice. Even though I begrudged giving her a penny to fritter away, I threw some money on the table before I left, and told her I would see her right. Better that way than have her going to the authorities for maintenance, and having some suit on my back asking stupid questions. I paid Joe a visit, and made sure he understood there would be trouble if he didn't keep his wife in order. How could he call himself a man if he couldn't even control one woman?

Time passed, life resumed its normal routine and the money continued to roll in. I told Sarah we needed to move to another flat as there were rumours we were under observation from the tax people. Why should we give our hard-earned money to the leeches? She argued a bit at first, then found a luxury place about ten miles out and happily made all the arrangements. The safe deposit box was bursting at the seams, even after paying out for fancy curtains and carpets for our new home. The girl had taste, and I couldn't help comparing it with the scruffy flat where my wife was bringing up my children. I visited them now and again when I needed to go back to London, but they were almost strangers to me now, and I wasn't exactly welcomed with open arms.

'Oh, it's you, the proverbial bad penny. What's brought you here?'

'That's a fine way to greet your husband and the father of your children.'

Just because I wasn't around 24/7 the woman was getting above herself, thinking she was the boss. After becoming used to my home at the coast, I looked around the small, dingy flat with distaste. What else should I expect from someone brought up in my peasant country, without a decent education? Comparing the two women I was supporting, the breeding of my English Rose stood out a mile, while my wife had let herself go, and although she still had a good figure her clothes were drab and she looked like an old woman.

'Here. Get your hair done and smarten yourself up a bit. You make me ashamed,' I said, throwing some money on the table. Although I was being generous, it was a pittance to what Sarah would spend on a new dress when I treated her. It just goes to show, class wins out. When Marija started her usual moans about the cost of children's clothes, I left her to it. What did she want from me? Blood? With two women to support she should be grateful I'd bothered to take the time to visit and give her some cash. After all, she wasn't contributing in any way, just take, take, take. That was women for you.

Chapter Eighteen

It was a relief to drive the Mercedes the eighty-odd miles home, and with the radio blaring out some decent soul and rock music, my good mood had been restored by the time I completed the two-hour journey, and I was ready for some action. As I opened the door Sarah came out of the bedroom, looking sexy and inviting in a black cocktail dress.

'Wow! That's the way to greet your man,' I told her, pulling her into my arms for a kiss. 'You look gorgeous, babe. Is that a new perfume?'

'Oh. Hi, TJ. Don't smudge my lipstick. I didn't expect you back yet. I was just on my way out.'

My grip on her arms tightened as hard as my erection.

'What do you mean you're going out? Is this what I get for trusting you alone for a few hours while I slave to keep you happy?'

'TJ, you're hurting me. Have you forgotten? You arranged it. George is back in town and you know he's one of my regular clients. I'm meeting him at his hotel and I'm already late.'

My temper faded as I remembered setting it up before I left. It was one thing for her to meet business clients and I shouldn't have jumped to conclusions. The marks on her arms should have faded by the time she met him, but even so I was willing to do my bit.

'Don't worry. Now I'm here I'll give you a lift to the hotel.'

Never let it be said that I didn't look after my woman. For some reason she didn't want me to escort her into the hotel, and I noted the pipsqueak on reception trying to look through the blacked-out windows when I stopped the car by the main entrance.

'Don't worry about picking me up,' she said as she sashayed through the revolving doors. 'I'll get a cab home. I'm not sure how long I'll be.'

'Make sure he pays extra if it's too late,' was my parting shot as I watched her suck up to the pimply youth on reception, before she called the lift to take her up to George's apartment. Despite my frustration, it started me thinking as I drove home. It wasn't right to be reliant on some kid who might have a big mouth, when I had worked so hard to set up the business. Hotels had been necessary to start, but now things were established I needed to take back some control.

Surprisingly, she was up for my idea of having an established base. We looked at some other apartments, close enough to be an easy journey, but far enough away to have no connection with our home. After a few months we found the perfect place. I would have gone for a cheaper flat near the docks, but she talked me out of it. The clientele would expect somewhere discreet, not near the rough seaman looking for a good time. The rent wasn't that expensive, despite being in the best part of town, on a block with mainly older residents who either never ventured out, or would be sound asleep by nine o'clock.

It needed a good deal of work but she had the vision. I withdrew from the savings box, and by the time the decorators had finished the place looked amazing.

Privacy, sophistication and no nosey neighbours. What more could we ask? The business took off and I realised it was a good move. Many of the prospective clients distrusted hotels as they involved too much trackable paperwork. This was perfect and the expenditure was repaid one hundred-fold.

Chapter Nineteen

Life was good. I'd come a long way from the illiterate country boy with the threat of the belt if the pigs weren't fed. Now I was a wheeler-dealer of the exclusive kind, negotiating deals and coming out on top. When I hit the casinos, it was as a regular punter rather than a scammer, so I had no hassles from security. Although it was not as lucrative as the con I had set up with Max, the bank box covered my losses and my IOUs were honoured, so I was greeted as a respectable businessman.

When you're on a roll, there's always something to bring you down. Just because it had been six months or more since I had seen my wife, she kicked up and caused problems. The word spread and eventually reached Sarah's ears. Living near the coast had its disadvantages as many of my countrymen had taken employment on the ships, and everyone was a distant relative with a nose for spreading gossip. Sarah went behind my back, made enquiries, discovered the truth and gave me an ultimatum. I made my choice, and the passing of the new law allowing divorce after two years' separation, made the process easier than it would have been only a short time before.

Although Marija had religious objections she knew when she was beaten, and after I promised to provide regular maintenance, signed the papers. The legal eagles took their exorbitant cut for preparing a few documents and I married Sarah. This was a far cry from the down-beat reception at my first wedding. Although it made a major dent in the bank balance, our guests were high-class and the champagne was genuine, not cheap imitation. I'd learnt from my mistakes of the past.

Sarah continued to be inventive in her work, and I was able to demand higher fees as her popularity increased. The other flat was put to good use, and our own place remained my private sanctuary. Occasionally I offered to go with her as protection when she had business appointments in the other apartment, but she reminded me that the main service the clients demanded was to be dominated, so there was little danger. She took on a maid to provide a reception service, and over time doubled the number of daily visitors.

At one stage I considered relocating back to London, but if we moved, we would have to start again building up the business with new patrons. Sex shops and clubs now riddled Soho, and rumours abounded that with corruption getting out of hand, the new commissioner intended to clean up the area. We were better off being the big fish in an area where we were established, and there was little or no competition. The tarts by the docks catered in back alleys for the rough sailors, but my set-up was discreet and unique. Then she delivered her bombshell. She was pregnant.

'What do you mean, you're expecting?' I demanded, my temper getting the better of me as I lashed out, catching her a stinging blow across the face. 'How many times do I have to tell you to always take precautions when you're working? You're an amenity, not a baby factory.'

'It's nothing like that, TJ,' she sobbed. 'I'm a Dom, not a cheap whore. As you'd know if you ever bothered to help, instead of spending all your time drinking and gambling.'

She needed to be taught a lesson, but as I took off my belt, she grabbed my arms.

'It's yours, TJ,' she sobbed. 'I've never been with anyone else. You're the father.'

Unknowingly her hand moved to her cheek, and I noticed the livid, red mark reaching from her jaw nearly to her left eye. If it left a bruise, it wouldn't be a good look for greeting the clients.

'Now, look what you made me do,' I said as I went to caress her face. She flinched and I noticed her other hand dropped to cover her belly. 'How are you going to work when you look like the back of a bus? If you wanted a kid you should have asked me first, not let yourself get up the duff without telling me. I need to sort out what to do when you can't work. How far gone are you?'

'It was that night you came back from the casino. You remember. You'd had a bad night, and I told you it wasn't safe but you insisted. It won't stop me working much. It would only be for the final few months. I'm sorry.'

I forgave her and although she carried on working until a few weeks before she gave birth to my son, I had to cut back on her expenditure. There was no point buying couture until she regained her figure, and it would be an expensive time for me. My son deserved the best. I insisted he had a traditional English name, but let her chose what to call our daughter who was born a few years later. Girls weren't important, but she redeemed herself when our third child was another boy.

At least this time I wasn't an unpaid baby sitter. Sarah made arrangements for a professional nanny to take care of our first-born when she went back to work. The nanny was a tasty young piece and after all, a man needed some satisfaction after going without when his wife was unable to fulfil her duties. She didn't stay long, but was replaced by an old bag who was fifty if she was a day. Even I had my limits. Perhaps Sarah's hormones had made her more suspicious, or perhaps she was becoming more worldly.

Either way, I kept the finances afloat until, after allowing her a short break, I told her it was time she returned to looking after the clients I worked so hard to provide. She complained of being tired, but with the children taken care of, she would have nothing better to do than sit around all day. In this business it was necessary to take up every opportunity and stay in the limelight. A long break would mean they would look elsewhere, and I would have to start again finding suitable punters. She wasn't being fair so I insisted. After all, it wasn't as if what she did was onerous.

After some persuasion she accepted the situation, but feigned exhaustion when I demanded my due as her husband. Who could blame me if her attitude meant I was obliged to obtain my satisfaction elsewhere? I was still young and virile and there was plenty on offer. Gradually the regulars returned, but I kept in touch with the trends and introduced new and inventive ways to keep them happy. Looking back, they were some of the best years. I was proud of my beautiful home, and the other property rental provided a steady income from the girls who worked there.

Chapter Twenty

The bank manager treated me as a valued customer and gave me sound financial advice. He had noticed the up and down pattern of my account, and although the safe deposit box was overflowing, told me slow and steady would invoke less attention, and improve my credit rating. To thank him, I treated him to several good meals in the best restaurants, and gave him a birthday bonus of a visit to one of my girls. He stopped asking prying questions and became a valuable ally. It was a whole new world from my father's idea of cash stuffed under the floorboards, but then I had moved on from being the country bumpkin and now looked on myself as a proper English gentleman. As usual it was a woman who upset the good life with her constant demands.

'What's wrong with you? When was the last time you welcomed me home with a smile? I should never have married you,' I told Sarah as I opened the door to what had become the usual long face.

'TJ, the children are growing up and the school are suspicious. This isn't the life a mother of three should be leading. The other mums talk about me behind my back.'

'Women always gossip, babe. Forget it. They're only jealous.'

'It's more than that. William came home today with a picture he had drawn. The teacher told the class to draw a picture of their mummy. All the others showed their mothers cooking or doing housework. His picture was of me with a whip in my hand. He must have seen something. I told them it was a feather duster but the looks they gave me. I know they didn't believe me.'

She turned on the waterworks and turned me off. Any thoughts of taking her to bed for some fun dwindled as quickly as the bulge in my pants. What was it with females? Were they never satisfied? They wanted a home, you gave them a home. They wanted kids, you gave them kids. You found them something to keep them occupied, easy money, doing what came naturally but were they happy? No! Always wanting something more, and less included to keep their man warm in bed after everything we did for them. At least the women in my village knew how to respect the head of the household. These English women had become spoilt, and thought they were an equal to the men in their lives. The blame lay fairly and squarely on the women's lib shit which was all the rage, and gave them ideas above their station.

We jogged along for a while and she knew better than to rile me when I was at home. The children were her responsibility. All I demanded was a meal on the table whenever I got in, and some peace in my own home. Occasionally I took my rights, but most of the time it wasn't worth the effort and my relief came from elsewhere. What had happened to the gorgeous, sexy lady who couldn't wait to take me to bed? As soon as she had a ring on her finger she changed from a vibrant, loving woman to a harridan shrew. At least she still had her looks and the clientele paid well.

They continued to provide me with a reasonable standard of living but I was becoming restless. I missed the buzz of the West End and the fast style of living. I'd been here long enough for all the best places to know me and welcome me as a valued customer, but I was bored. There were few new faces, most of the available girls had been tasted, and a repeat performance was never as exciting as the first time. My second wife made good money from her looks, but she also had a good brain.

'TJ,' she said to me one night, when I was feeling particularly down after a disappointing evening. 'You always say the restaurants around here have no class. How about opening our own? We could find a Paris trained chef, and you could run it. We'd make it exclusive and people would come from miles around. I know many of my clients would support it, and if we only opened in the evenings, I'd have more time to spend with the children during the day. They're growing up so fast and I'm missing the best years of their lives. We hardly see each other these days. We could become a proper family with a respectable business.'

It was worth considering. With the cream of society as my guests, I would be esteemed and respected, able to hold my head up with none of the derisive sniggering aimed at the sleazy club owners.

'I'll think about it,' I told her. 'It's not a bad idea but I'll have to find the right place, in a decent area. I don't want the riffraff thinking just because they can afford it, they'd be welcome.'

That night she returned to being the sexy, exciting woman I had married. Her job had taught her how to keep a man happy, and she pulled out all the stops. All it needed was a firm hand and everything was as it should be. I didn't give much thought to her idea over the following few months. My priority was keeping the business up to date, finding new clients and making the occasional visit to London to discover what was new in the real world, rather than languishing in the sticks. Soho had changed a lot, and many of my cronies had moved out of the old ways and taken up jobs as cab drivers or labourers with the council.

Chapter Twenty-one

'It's a different world now, TJ,' a friend from the old days told me when we met in his club for a drink. 'Never mind the Swinging 60s, if it's not the strikes it's women's lib. Gone are the days when they knew their place. What with all the foreigners, Chinky restaurants and Raymond buying up everywhere, it's hard for the boys to make a living. There's not the money around, and who's going to risk being blown up for the sake of a few blues, or a bit of skirt when it's available everywhere for nothing? You did the right thing getting out. How's life treating you down by the coast? My missus keeps nagging me to move out of London now the kids are growing up. It's not the same anymore, and we're all getting older.'

'It's good,' I told him. 'She's class, not like the scrubbers round here, and the punters are the best. You wouldn't believe the number of judges and councillors on my books. And they don't expect freebies, they pay good money and keep their mouths shut. I'm thinking of expanding and opening a restaurant. Only the best. Just got to find the right place. I'll let you know when I'm up and running, and you and a few of the boys can come down and have a decent meal on me. It'll be like old times.'

It seemed like an omen. When I returned home the following day, Sarah rushed to the door to greet me.

'TJ. Guess what? I've found the perfect place. Horace told me about it when I saw him for our usual session yesterday. It was a restaurant before but with the way the economy's going they went bankrupt. We can easily afford the price they're asking, and still have plenty left over to do it up. He's offered to sort out the legal stuff for us and the auctions next week, but if we put our bid in now, he can swing it in our favour. He took me to see it yesterday. Just think, we could be open for Christmas. The New Year could see the start of our new life.'

'Whoa, slow down woman. I haven't even seen it yet and I don't like the idea of someone else being involved. Tell me where it is, and if it's any good I'll check out the bank tomorrow and see where I stand. For now, I'm hungry, tired and need some loving. Once all my needs are satisfied, I'll be able to think straight.'

The following morning, I looked in the safe deposit box to find it was crammed full. Not with low denomination notes either, only the big stuff, and proper modern decimalised notes, not old-fashioned fivers. I had done well to keep Mr Williams, the bank manager, sweet. Although my bank statement only showed enough to keep the tax man happy, he had advised me to replace my 'rainy-day' supply with the new currency. It came to light when I treated him to a meal and tried to pay with an old banknote. The cashier made a fuss, and if Williams hadn't been there to smooth things over, I would have rammed the note down the throat of the pompous little nobody. My money was as good as anybody's. I didn't want the banker to know how much I had, but instructed Sarah to take out small wads and change them at various outlets over a period of time so as not to cause suspicion. It wasn't right she had access to the box, but I needed her experience to deal with the mundane things, while I decided on the future.

The restaurant site was about ten miles out, at the end of a short leafy lane, plenty of parking space, secluded and with enough grounds for summer parties. The building was spacious and sound, although the décor was old-fashioned. It reminded me in some ways of my father's bakery, but with some modern equipment and decent furniture it should do well.

'I've been to look at the restaurant,' I told Sarah when I arrived home. 'You'll need to start sorting the legal stuff if it's to open by Christmas. There's a lot to do but with my contacts I can make it work. Go and see the solicitor in the morning, then find some proper furniture. The stuff in there is out of the arc. My place is going to be class. Order only the best but don't let them rip you off.'

'Oh, TJ! Do you mean it? That's wonderful. I can't wait to start running a respectable business. It'll be the making of us, and good for the children too.'

'Hold on, woman. Since when was it *your* business? You just sort the mundane equipment and let me take care of the important things, as a man should. Whoever heard of a woman running a successful business? Now come and show me how grateful you are.'

Chapter Twenty-two

We could have made a go of it too and lived a respectable life, except I had never lost my gambling habit. Easy come, easy go. Once I was back in the money the betting drug took over, so the more she earned the more I raided the safe deposit box. If only my luck had turned, the restaurant would have had the best of everything, all paid for up-front. I didn't believe in mortgages and buying second-rate, but time was not on my side.

When she went to arrange the deposit, she found the box empty. I had intended to pay it back but she never told me she would need some cash before the purchase was finalised. A few more weeks and it would have been fine, I would have been back on a winning streak and she would never have known. She should have warned me.

I had never seen her so angry. It took all my skills and charm to get her to cool down. Even then she was moody and turned her back on me when we went to bed. I put up with her tantrums for a while then decided I'd had enough. The next time she tried turning away I took her anyhow. After all she was my wife and it was her duty to satisfy her husband. When I fell asleep she got out of bed and went into the spare room. Let her sulk. Maybe next time she would realise I was still the master of my own house and do as she was told.

I did my best to win some back so she could put down the deposit, even if it was overdue. Nothing had been signed officially so I couldn't see the problem, despite her nagging about someone else getting in first and buying it. I'd told the guy I wanted it so why all the fuss? Were they saying my word wasn't good enough? It was my restaurant so the pen pushers better not think of going behind my back. They'd get their money when I was good and ready.

At first the cards ran in my favour and the wad of notes felt good in my pocket. I had been playing all day, but decided to have a few more hands to give me enough to repay what I had taken, and add a bit on top. I was tired but my last poker hand of the day was a good one. There were only two of us left in the game so I went for broke.

I lost.

Throwing down my cards I drove home in a bad temper. I'd spent the whole day trying to do right by her, but when I asked what was for dinner, she had the cheek to tell me to make it myself! Well, if that didn't deserve a slap I don't know what did. I ignored her crocodile tears and went up for a shower and to change my clothes. The size of the bruise on her cheek took me by surprise, but then I realised it was her own fault for winding me up when I was down. She should have been supporting me, not turning against me.

Without another word I went out, slamming the door behind me, and drove to see a bloke I knew who could lend me a few quid. Okay his interest rates were high but I could pay it back when my luck turned again, even if he wasn't the type to mess about. With some money in my pocket, I drove to a club for a few drinks to unwind. I hadn't intended to stay long but some friends arrived and it turned into a bit of a celebration.

'Put your money away, TJ. Everything's on me tonight. That sweet little filly in the 3.30 did me proud. Gawd bless her. Right, what's everyone drinking?'

Naturally I couldn't let him show me up, so I put my hand in my pocket more than he did. Five girls turned up that someone knew vaguely, and the rounds of drinks came faster and progressively more expensive. It felt good to have some fun again, even if the stash in my pocket slimmed done as the evening went on. There was still enough left, and tomorrow could take care of itself. The sexiest girl from the group was giving me the eye, and making it obvious she fancied me. She was a real looker, so when a fast number came on, I dragged her up to dance.

Whether it was the frustration of recent events, the drink, the music or a bit of each, I let loose and showed her exactly how I had earned my reputation. She was a great dancer and we got faster and wilder. The applause when we sat down made me feel good for the first time that day. She sat on my lap and didn't object when I slipped my hand under her mini skirt and let it rest on her thigh. When the music slowed I got her up to dance again, and felt just how big and firm her breasts were. The club closed at 3 a.m. so we piled into my car to go back to the flat she shared with one of the other girls. I dragged Charlie along even though he was so drunk he could hardly stand.

Somehow the four of us got there without smashing the car up, and we stumbled up the stairs and all fell into the bedroom the girls shared. It wasn't a problem as they both had double beds. I took my girl to her bed while Charlie got in with the other one. The drink and company didn't put me off and I soon had her squealing. After second helpings I took a break and noticed the other girl watching us. Charlie had fallen asleep and was snoring loudly, so I called her over to join us. For a while I let the girls pleasure me until my libido was restored and I was able to service them both. Then I slept for an hour before driving home.

Chapter Twenty-three

It was gone seven when I got in and my wife was up cooking breakfast. After a big fry-up I went back to bed to catch up on some sleep. She didn't speak to me apart from saying I stunk of drink. When I got up the house was empty- just like my pocket. I wasn't certain if I had spent all the money I had borrowed, or if the girls had helped themselves. Going through my wife's underwear drawer I found the secret stash she kept there. All I needed was some readies to keep me going for a while. She came into the bedroom as I was getting dressed and her eyes went straight to the partially open drawer. Checking the now empty packet she turned to glare at me.

'Have you no shame?' she snivelled.

'Do you want another black eye to match?' I yelled as I went out, slamming the door in temper. She had no right to keep things hidden from me. She was the one always going on about marriage being a partnership, but with her it seemed to be a one-way street. Without me she would have nothing. I drove to the dog track and finally my luck changed for the better. After winning slowly but steadily for a while, I cleaned up with an accumulator and made a bundle. I considered going home and throwing it in her face to prove she should have had more trust in me. Then common sense prevailed.

'TJ. Good to see you,' the money lender greeted me. 'The boys wanted to pay you a reminder visit, but I told them you were a man of your word. Come and have a drink while we square up the account. I assume that's why you're here.'

His three thugs surrounded me but he waved them off as we went through to somewhere more private. I'd made the right decision; these were not guys to mess with. I paid him part of my winnings; not enough to clear the debt completely but sufficient to keep him sweet for a while. With the money I had left I thought about going home, but then realised the need to build up my reserves so decided to head for the club. There was a game going; only small stakes but enough for a start. My luck held out and after a couple of hours' play I was well up on the night, and had even recovered the sum I had paid off from my debt. It crossed my mind to go back and clear the rest but I needed some readies. Popping into a local bar for a quick one before going home early, I noticed Charlie sitting in a corner with his girl from the other night.

'Hey, Charlie. Good to see you, mate. What are you both drinking?'

'We're fine thanks. Just got one in. In fact, we were leaving anyway.'

'One for the road,' I insisted, but again he refused my offer, and soon after they got up and left. Maybe she was embarrassed after our three in a bed romp. Women! Who can understand them? She wasn't complaining at the time, but now she'd gone all little miss innocent. They were welcome to each other. The place was quiet as it was still early, and I was tempted to down my drink and go home when a woman sitting on her own caught my eye. She was sitting on one of the high bar stools, and her short skirt was riding nicely up her thighs giving a glimpse of stocking tops. Deciding it might be worth hanging around for a while I took the seat next to her.

'Hi, I'm TJ, and your glass is nearly empty. Barman, a large one for me and the same for the lady. Have one yourself and keep the change,' I said throwing down a £1 note.

'Oh, thanks,' she said attempting to pull down her skirt without success. I noticed she didn't give me her name and she seemed a bit nervous, constantly glancing at the door.

'Were you expecting someone?' I asked, following her gaze.

'No, no it's fine. Sorry. Thanks for the drink. I'm pleased you turned up.'

I leaned in for a better look down the front of her top, and draped my arm across her back before letting it drop to give her bum a squeeze. Although she glanced at the door again, she didn't push my hand away so it seemed I was on a winner tonight. It got complicated when my girl from the other night turned up with a man in tow, and I recognised him as one of the local villains. He came over to say hello and bought a drink for me and the girl with me. I nodded briefly to acknowledge his woman, but not being sure of their relationship didn't make it obvious I knew her.

Surprisingly, she brought up the subject of the night we had spent together and started talking about it in an over-loud voice. She was already drunk and I didn't want any problems from the guy with her. At first, I tried to laugh it off, but then just to shut her up, admitted it. As if to stake her claim the girl from the bar draped herself over me, and I pulled her onto my lap and gave her a deep snog as a sign of things to come. My hands were wandering, but as we came up for air, I found myself looking straight into the face of my wife. I was shocked when she didn't go for the girl on my lap, but gave the other woman a punch that would have made Sonny Liston proud.

Chapter Twenty-four

'That's for what you did with my husband, you slut,' she screamed, clawing her nails down the girl's face.

Turning on her heels Sarah marched out, closely followed by the girl from the bar, who extricated herself from my lap and took off after my wife. At first, I was too stunned to move but as I went to follow them out, I saw through the glass door Sarah talking with the girl who five minutes before had been offering me her body. She passed some money to the woman who put it in her bag, then after a quick conversation they hugged each other before both going their separate ways.

What the f… was going on? Catching up with my wife I forced her into the car and drove home to find out. Once we were inside, she tried to go off to the spare bedroom but I pulled her back.

'What was that all about?' I yelled at her. 'Can't a man have a quiet drink in peace? What were you doing in that bar anyway? How dare you follow me?' I was blustering as I knew I had been caught out but for once she turned on me.

'You bastard!' she screamed. 'People told me but I didn't believe them. I only went along with Charlie's idea to stop all the gossip and prove you innocent. I must have been blind to believe all your lies. You'll never change. Anything in a skirt and you're up for it, never mind your wife and kids at home. I've had enough. I just can't take any more.'

With that she rushed off to the spare bedroom and this time I let her go. For a while after that the atmosphere in the house could be cut with a knife. She made my meals, did my washing but only spoke to me if it was absolutely necessary. She didn't come to my bed and in a way I was glad. How could I get it up when the only thing to greet me was a sour face? I gave the clubs a miss for a while and was home at a reasonable time most nights. I needn't have bothered. When I got in she was already in bed and I started to miss the sex and the loving woman I had married. It also worried me whether the nasty piece of work who was with the girl she had thumped would be looking for retribution. Why did women have to interfere and cause problems? If she'd stayed at home, none of this would have happened.

To add to my worries, my luck deserted me and I found myself losing heavily. When I went to the safe deposit box, it was empty and my temper exploded. There should have been plenty of cash as I hadn't been near it for a while, so one of the thieving bastards from the bank must have been helping themselves. I insisted on seeing Mr Williams, the manager, but learnt he had moved to another branch, and the sour old codger who ushered me into his office didn't show me the same respect as his predecessor.

'Sir, my staff have no access to your private box. Only you and your wife have the keys so I would be obliged if you would cease making unfounded allegations. If you want to know the full circumstances, I suggest you cool down, return home and discuss it with your wife. We have your signed document confirming joint and several authority, and as such, are authorised to accept her instructions.'

'Don't give me all that legal shit. She's my wife so it's my money. No way any bitch would dare steal from me. Now, what are you going to do about it?'

'I would be obliged if you would modify your language, sir. As I've explained, your wife has the full right to transfer the funds to her own name, in accordance with your signed mandate. Frankly, seeing your attitude today I don't blame her, but the bank has acted totally in compliance with instructions.'

'What are you saying? She's put it in another box? Why didn't you say so, instead of giving me so much grief? Just fetch me the new box and I can check if it's all there.'

'I'm sorry sir. You have no right of access to the other box.'

'I'm her husband. Get the key now if you know what's good for you.' Just when I was starting to relax, he had wound me up again, and my temper exploded. As I stood up he reached for what was obviously some sort of alarm under his desk.

'If you don't leave immediately, I'm calling the police.' He would have too, the little weasel.

My only option was to go back to the money lender. With the rest of the last loan added to the new one, and a higher interest rate, I needed to make some money, and fast. Taking wild chances put me even deeper into debt. It was all Sarah's fault. If she hadn't made such a fuss, I would have been able to concentrate and recoup my losses. The missed repayments built up and I was worried. No one would accept my IOUs as I had gained the reputation as a welcher. Things were going from bad to worse, and my usual positive attitude deserted me. I needed to have it out with Sarah, and get access to some of the cash she had squirreled away.

The house seemed quiet when I arrived home, but then I heard sobbing coming from the bedroom. I found her lying face down on the bed and pulled her round to ask what was wrong. Her face gave me the answer. It was a mess. Looking round I noticed the havoc; broken glass and smashed objects were strewn everywhere. All the stupid ornaments she loved were in thousands of pieces on the floor.

'Three gorillas left a message for you. They said the next reminder for your overdue payment won't be so pleasant. I was terrified,' she sobbed. 'They held a knife to my face and told me how pretty I was -for now!'

Even though I had let her down, the next evening she thrust a packet into my hands and told me to make sure it went straight to paying off my debt. I did, and for a while kept to the straight and narrow. Knowing most of the cash from the safe deposit box had gone to clear our debts, I threw myself into getting more clients for her, so we could be comfortable again. All went well for a while and although there was not much left over, the bills were paid and life was stable, if not exciting. After a few months, the gambling fever took over again, although this time I made sure to stay clear of the money lenders.

She left me.

Chapter Twenty-five

She wasn't completely to blame. It wasn't just the money she had worked so hard for; I had lost her trust and put the kids at risk. What sort of low-life scum would threaten a woman and children for the sake of a measly few quid? As a single man again, I went back to my old lifestyle. Being a naval area there were plenty of sailors. Where there were sailors there were girls, and where there were girls, well, that was what I knew best. Except these weren't class escorts, but cheap back-alley working girls, ready to do anything for a few bob. The money they earned was scarcely enough for me to keep my head above water, and the clientele were rough and most often drunk, making my job protecting them so much more difficult. I missed the soft, respectable business clients who wanted nothing more than decent champagne and a beautiful woman ready to indulge their fantasies.

Although I wasn't in debt to the heavies, I ran out of friends willing to sub me short term loans when the horses let me down. Several of the local bookies black-listed me and word spread. I was watched like a hawk in the casinos, and made to feel unwelcome at even the playing-for-peanuts card games. With nothing left for me by the coast I decided to high-tail it back to London. The provincial life was stifling me and I needed a change, but somehow even Soho had lost its glitter and charm.

'Well, Look what the wind's blown in,' one of the guys greeted me as I paid a visit to the old club. 'How's it going, TJ? Haven't seen you in many a year. Still chasing the ladies?'

'Watch your mouth, Mario, before I teach you to speak with no teeth. Where is everyone? Who are all these young kids? It's like the bloody United Nations in here.'

'No offence, TJ. Things have changed a lot. All the old boys have gone, but I did bump into Frankie the other day, and we were wondering how you were. The boss is still around, but I don't think you'll know anyone else.'

'Tell him I'm here, will you, and get me a large one.'

'Sure, but keep it out of sight. These council idiots are a bugger for staying within licencing hours. Not like the old days when they put more down their neck than any of the regular punters. I'll give the boss a shout, he's in his office.'

'TJ. Good to see you, man,' Joe said as he recognised me. 'Come on through and bring your drink with you. To what do I owe the honour of this visit?'

'Just paying a neighbourly call, Joe,' I said as I sat down facing him. 'I'm back in the smoke for a while to drum up some business. The sticks have been good, but there's nothing like being in the centre of the action. Mind you, it looks a lot different now.'

'Tell me about it. All these different nationalities flooding in and taking over. You don't know the half of it. The fuzz on our backs all the time in their clean up Soho campaign. You can't even rely on the council now. At one time the authority figures were happy to top up their wages with a few sweeteners to give us a tip-off, but now it's all University pen-pushers. Little trumped-up pip-squeaks, all of them. To be honest, I'd like to chuck it all in and retire to the country somewhere. Times have changed and there's too much competition now.'

'What about the deliveries, Joe? With all these hippies about, there must be some money in that. I could help you out while I'm here. You know you can trust me to do a good job.'

'There's a supplier on every street corner now, TJ. Even the films are hard to sell with all this free love everywhere. Nowadays they're more likely to sit at home watching TV or going to the flicks. I'd like to help you out but it's hard enough to pay the bills, let alone take on another drain for the old cash-flow.'

'I didn't come here to bum off you, Joe,' I said, trying to keep my temper under control. 'I'm doing alright, just wanted to say hello to an old friend, and see how you were getting on. Well, I'd better get off. Lots of business to sort. Sorry things aren't going so well for you.'

With that I stormed out. Fair enough he'd been good to me in the early days, but there was always something around the corner for someone like me who could move with the times and was open to opportunities. The years passed and I stayed in London, but the flat I found was a far cry from the luxury place I'd had at the coast. Time had turned full circle but at least the one-bedroomed place I rented in Wandsworth had easy access to the West End, and was in the heart of the community where many of my compatriots had settled.

I was no longer a young man, and the only job I could get was sweeping floors, cleaning up and running errands. Not the lucrative errands I used to do; now it was just going to the corner shop to get someone a packet of cigarettes or a bottle of wine. Age and the excesses of life were catching up with me. I suffered from the cold and damp and even the summer didn't help my arthritis.

Sometimes I thought of my children from my two marriages. They must be grown up now, but had no contact with me. My second wife did manage to track me down, if only to serve me with divorce papers. She wanted to get married again, and after a fraught meeting with her legal eagles I settled for a lot less than was my due. After a while she divorced me, remarried, and I didn't see my children again. My home was now a small dingy flat similar to the one I had when I first moved to London. Some of the boys who remembered me from the old days had made their fortune and ensured I didn't starve. It was not my way to accept charity but now I had no choice.

My hair turned grey but unlike some of the old boys, I never went bald, and it stayed curly until I had it cut. I never lost my love of music, and it only took a bit of Rock and Roll before I forgot my aches and pains and gave it all I'd got. The youngsters had nothing on me. A beautiful woman still caught my eye, but now they treated me like a favourite grandfather, rather than a prospective lover. Time catches up with the best of us, but the spirit was willing even if the body was no longer up to it.

Chapter Twenty-six

I didn't go back to my village to show off in a luxury car- but I did go back.

Perhaps our heritage is ingrained in our nature more than we think. I'm here now, in the square, sitting in the sunshine with the other old men; watching the young girls go by and the young boys ogling them. I've become something of a celebrity as most of the men my age have never left the village. When I'm in the mood I regale them with my stories of the limousine and riches I left behind. They listen enthralled when I tell them of the life I led, the girls I had, and the money I spent; often more in one evening than they would see in a lifetime.

I didn't forget how to speak English, and although our village was not one of the tourist high-spots, we did get the occasional visitors. It was the beautiful blonde girl who first caught my attention, when she and the man with her took the table outside the café, near where I was sitting with the old fogies by the church. The young guy seemed to be listening to what I was saying, even though our language was little known outside the island, apart from the areas in Australia and Canada where some of the more adventurous had emigrated.

Bored with the adulation of the traditional old cronies, I wanted the company of the young and vibrant sightseers, so recognising their London accents I passed them on the pretext of going into the café.

'Hi. Welcome to our village. How are you enjoying your holiday?' I asked them in English. 'Are you from London? I lived there for many years.'

The girl gave me a beaming smile. If only I'd been thirty years younger.

'Hello. Lovely to meet you. I can't get over how friendly everyone is here. Yes, we're from London. This is my fiancé, Will, and I'm Jane. His family is from around here, so it's a bit of a nostalgia trip for him, but it's the first time I've visited your lovely island. Actually, you look a bit alike. I wonder if you're distantly related?'

For the first time I took proper notice of her companion, and saw many of my own features looking back at me. The same curly hair I had at his age, the slim hips I could imagine moving to some upbeat music, and the same desire to explore the world and make something of himself. The look he gave me showed something of his darker side, and reminded me of my own father.

'We've seen everything we came to see, Jane. Time to move on, I think.' His voice sounded sad but angry at the same time. 'I hope you achieved your dreams, sir but I doubt we will meet again. Jane, I'll go in and pay the bill. Meet you back at the car.'

He stood up and went inside, leaving his girlfriend looking at me with a puzzled expression, as if it was unusual for her man to be so ungracious. To save her embarrassment I took her hand and gave her a gallant kiss.

'I apologise if Will sounded rude; it's very unlike him. Normally he's the sweetest, kindest man you could imagine. The only time he gets upset is talking about his family. His father deserted them when he was young, and he's never got over it. Anyway, it's been lovely meeting you. I'm sorry, I didn't catch your name.'

'My name would mean nothing to him,' I told her. 'In the old days everyone was known by a nickname, but times change. I'm sorry too. I would have liked to get to know you both better. Goodbye, my lovely lady. Take care of your man, but make sure he treats you right.'

With that I rose and returned to the old men eagerly waiting to hear more of my stories. With them I had the respect I deserved, and they sought out my company to hear my tales. I am important and revered. Even if I've loved and lost, gone from poverty to money to burn, and back again, I've never lost my pride. I escaped from being an illiterate country boy and became someone who wore designer clothes, and ate in the best restaurants in one of the greatest cities in the world.

Now I'm back where I belong but the memories…I will always have the memories, and they grow wilder and more extravagant with each passing year.

Reviews.

If you enjoyed this book PLEASE consider leaving a review, and telling your friends. It's a great way of helping other readers find books they might enjoy, and is an invaluable resource to authors.
Grateful thanks go to book bloggers who give up their time to help spread the word.

Did you know?
You don't have to have purchased the book through Amazon to be able to leave a review there.
Reviews don't have to be complicated. The number of reviews is important so just a few words would be appreciated.
5 reviews will buy 1 ounce of fairy dust.
10 reviews will feed a Unicorn for a week.
50 reviews and Amazon will bring the book to the attention of a wider audience.
100 reviews provide the authors with the magic key to other worlds so they can write more stories for your enjoyment.

On behalf of authors everywhere *Thank you.*

More about the author.

You can find more details about the author and her other books by checking out her author pages and social media sites:

Amazon
www.amazon.com/Voinks/e/B01MVB8WNC

www.amazon.co.uk/Val-Portelli/e/B01MVB8WNC

Goodreads
www.goodreads.com/author/list/16843817.Val_Portelli

Web sites and blogs
www.Voinks.wordpress.com
www.quirkyunicornbooks.wordpress.com/val-portelli

Facebook
www.facebook.com/Voinks.writer.author

Printed in Great Britain
by Amazon